Dancing and Disaster

Modern Magick, 11

Charlotte E. English

1

THE JUMPING *PAS DE sissonne* was lovely, but it wasn't until Jay executed a passable *saut de basque sodecha* that I knew we were likely to win. He soared about six feet up (aided, conceivably, by a wee touch of levitation magick), performed a three-sixty-degree pirouette in mid-air *while doing the splits,* I mean, I ask you. Who could possibly top that?

Not our opponents, anyway. No chance.

'Let's not get too comfortable,' I warned a winded and sweating Jay. 'More to come.'

Jay hadn't the breath to speak, but the look he gave me said enough.

'Not yet,' I said, soothingly. 'Rest first.'

I waited, with a hopeful smile, as Jay fought for breath. When, at last, he stopped gasping for air, he said, 'No. No. Next time's your turn.'

'That's fair,' I said, cautious-like.

'I want a double *tour en l'air*, at *least*, Ves.'

'No can do.'

Jay looked at me.

'I might be able to go as high as a single.'

'Ves, I've just performed any number of manoeuvres of which *I am not capable* and my poor body will be paying for it for weeks.'

'Sorry,' I said, momentarily shame-faced. 'But you looked *fine*.'

Jay was not mollified. 'Double *tour en l'air*.'

'Okay.' I was meek and contrite. 'Anything for you.'

Jay shook his head. 'I'd ask how we even got here,' he panted, turning away from me. 'But what would be the point? We followed Ves. *That's* how we got here.'

Since you might be wondering the same sort of thing, permit me to explain myself.

It wasn't *entirely* my fault. Honest.

THE REGULATOR IS READY.

October came. Mid October, when the intense heat of summer had finally packed itself off and I'd spent several weeks as an apprentice to Merlin (yes, *the* Merlin, even if she wasn't quite as most of us expected). It was going pretty well, but we weren't done, not by a long shot.

Time waits for no man, however, and neither does Orlando, for the rumours started to circulate. *The regulator is ready.*

It's supposed to be a top-secret project, of course, so there shouldn't have been hearsay. Where there's life there's gossip, though, and there's plenty of life at the Society.

'Is it true?' I asked Milady. She hadn't summoned me. I'd invited myself, clambered all the way up the stairs to her tower-top room, knocked on the door, then waited over half an hour for an invitation to enter.

What can I say. I'd spent weeks and *weeks* at Home, and, while I'd had the by no means uninteresting diversion of Tuesdays at Merlin's cottage to entertain me, I was starting to get antsy. I was brimming with a small fortune in magick and I had nothing much to spend it on.

I'm a tool. *Use me.*

'I require more information in order to answer your question, Ves,' said Milady. 'Is what true?'

'You know what I mean.' I said this in a half-whisper, aware that I was dealing in information contraband.

Milady did not dignify this comment with an answer.

I kicked at the rich, blue carpet with one toe, feeling uncharacteristically annoyed. 'The regulator,' I said, capitulating. 'I hear it's ready.'

'Oh? And where did you hear that?'

I had to think for a second. 'Not Indira, of course. She's far too good to break faith with Orlando. But Nell mentioned it at lunch. And Luke at breakfast. And I heard Molly and Dave H. talking about it in the common room. Oh, and Aki said—'

'I see.' Milady sounded weary. The Society might be full of brilliant people doing important work, but we were like a bunch of rowdy, recalcitrant children sometimes. Poor Milady's hair must be grey to the last strand. I heard her take a deep breath. 'Officially, I can confirm nothing.'

'Of course.'

'But off the record, yes. Orlando has recently informed me that he has a functional prototype and he feels it will soon be time to test it in the field.'

Test it in the field. Words to strike delight into the heart of a Ves, and probably a Jay, too. Maybe. Hopefully. I bounced a bit on my toes. 'I volunteer!'

'I am well aware of your right of interest in this matter, Ves.'

That wasn't *quite* a yes. I frowned. 'You... you are planning to send me on this mission, aren't you?'

'How are your studies with Ophelia progressing?'

Not an answer. This didn't bode well.

'Excellently,' I said, with perfect truth. 'She's very patient with me.'

I make myself sound like a difficult student, but I'm not, not really. Not in the usual fashion. I am just eager, and brimming with enthusiasm, and I want to know everything *yesterday*. One cannot learn all of Merlin's myriad and ancient arts by last Tuesday, however, even with the best will in the world. Ophelia-who-is-Merlin bears gracefully with my impatience. Usually.

'I am reluctant to suspend your studies at this time,' said Milady.

My heart sank.

'It would only be for a little while!'

'It may not be. Your future role as Merlin is important.'

'So's the regulator! And who better than Jay and me to test it? We've been part of this from the beginning. We know everything about it. Who could possibly do a better job?'

'No one, Ves, that I grant you. Nonetheless—'

'Please,' I interrupted. 'Please?' My heart was dropping through the floor, and I was becoming seriously worried that Milady might leave me out. Might even send Jay and Indira without me.

There are times when I'll beg, if I have to. I'm not proud.

'I will consider the matter.'

I hoped I didn't imagine the slight softening of her tone.

Pity that she's a disembodied voice. I couldn't read her face to determine how sympathetic she was to my cause.

'I'll be on my best behaviour,' I promised. 'Strictly no shenanigans.'

Well, it wasn't really a lie. I said it in good faith. At the time.

To be honest with you, I'd said my studies with Ophelia were going well, but it's a little hard to gauge my actual progress.

She wasn't really teaching me anything solid. It's not like there's a set curriculum for Merlinhood, with a couple of exams at the end, so I know when I'm ready. She was teaching me along more abstract, wishy-washy — one might even say *airy-fairy* — lines, like: how to go deep with myself, so I truly know where I'm at and what I'm capable of. How to sense and manipulate my own magick, on a far deeper and more complex level than I've ever even heard of before. How to understand my own capacity — and safely exceed it, at need. How to sense and manipulate magick external to myself. How to draw on the world around me. And a fair bit of what one might call *magickal ethics*, according to Ophelia's admittedly peculiar world view.

It's not quite what they teach you at the University.

I'm already a far better practitioner than I used to be. I used to need a little magickal Curio to change the colour of my hair, as simple a thing as that is. I don't need such tools now, to the probable relief of Ornelle at Stores. The number of objects I need to, er, *borrow* from the Society's stockroom in order to do my job has drastically decreased.

But when it comes to Merlin's arts, the small stuff is inconsequential. Ophelia is teaching me to handle big stuff with big magick and I have no idea when that process will be complete.

To be even more honest, I'm not in a hurry for that day to come. Eventually, she'll decide I'm ready, even for the *really big stuff*. I'll be given the keys to all the ancient magick she possesses, trusted to use my powers for Good, not for Evil, and then... she'll disappear.

Leaving me to fight the good fight for British magick without her guidance.

Gulp.

Maybe I wasn't sorry for the prospect of a temporary suspension of study. It's been an overwhelming few months. I've changed in ways I never imagined possible. I'm wielding far more magick — and far more responsibility — than I know what to do with.

It'd be nice to put it all down for a week or two and go back to being Just Ves again. Just a field agent with the Society for Magickal Heritage, surrounded by my excellent and capable peers, achieving remarkable things in unorthodox ways and making stuff happen.

Blissful thought.

I wanted to talk about it.

Jay was out on a research trip with Melissa's team again, so I couldn't bitch at him about the unspeakable trials of my life.

Val was closeted with Merlin's grimoire, the loan of which I had successfully negotiated with Ophelia and Crystobel Elvyng. I had thereby secured Val's Eternal Gratitude for myself, which was no inconsiderable blessing. I had by the same means lost her attention for the foreseeable future, which was a pity.

I could go and talk to Rob. I've been doing that quite a lot, lately. He's a good friend and a good doctor and he has a nice, calming way about him that's very much appreciated in a crisis.

I've also had a few appointments with Grace, our head-rearranger, and she's excellent too. But they both use words like *anxiety* and *coping systems* rather a lot (usually prefaced with words like "unhealthy"). Much as I appreciate their help, their approach is medical rather than friendly; they treat my conditions rather than sympathising with my plight. If I wanted someone to bitch with, Rob wasn't going to be the ideal choice.

So, I went down to the Toil and Trouble division.

2

'You look like a parti-coloured rain cloud,' was Zareen's comment upon my appearance at her door.

She has a little cupboard of a room in the west wing, sort of near the library. It stood empty for over a month while Zareen was off enduring — er, *benefiting from* — her own, post-mission treatment back at the School of Weird. If I've had a tough time of it lately, try talking to Zar. By the end of a certain few, chaotic weeks, she was half out of her wits and I hadn't seen the whites of her eyes in a while.

She's better now. I think.

'I'm grumpy,' I agreed, plopping down into the only unoccupied chair in Zareen's tiny little room. I produced a few raindrops in illustration of my point, and they rained with cheerful greyness all over the faded crimson carpet.

'Let me guess...'

She was lounging in her chair as was her usual wont, her booted feet up on a corner of her disordered desk. The green streaks in her black hair were brighter than usual; freshly dyed. She'd lost the inky shadows under her eyes, mostly, and she was a normal-for-her kind of pale, not bone-white.

Most of all, she'd got her withering sarcasm back, as she proceeded to demonstrate.

'Word is the regulator's ready for testing, which ought to please you. But you're not pleased. So, you're officially too special and important to be sent out with it, is that it? Poor Ves.'

I glowered at her. 'Milady's reluctant to interrupt my studies.'

'With Merlin. *The* actual, literal Merlin, with whom many a person would kill to study.'

This is what I like about Zareen. She's bracingly realistic.

'You make a good point,' I allowed.

'I'll swap places with you.' She laughed at the look on my face, showing off a new tongue stud: poison-green and glittering. 'Not for real. It's not like Ophelia wouldn't notice.'

'No, that's actually a great idea,' I said earnestly. 'Merlin's got such a lot to teach. Everybody should benefit from it. Not just me.'

'Said in no selfish spirit whatsoever.'

'Zero self-interest involved,' I agreed. 'Not one iota.'

Zareen shrugged. 'I wouldn't say no to a lecture or two, but good luck getting it past Ophelia. And Milady.'

Ophelia was rather retiring. Curiously so, for a person with her kind of power. She was obviously most comfortable in her own cottage, teaching one person at a time (preferably me). She wasn't the type to volunteer herself as a lecturer.

I had a notion Milady might like the idea, however.

'Wouldn't get me out of Tuesdays, though,' I said, regretfully. 'I want only one glorious, glittering week...'

'Risking your life for the good of Queen and Country?'

'See. You get me.'

Zareen shook her head. 'Ves. Can you think of even a single time someone has seriously said no to you?'

I sat up a bit. 'Loads. Milady often says—'

She held up a hand. 'I'll rephrase. One single time someone has seriously said no to you, and you didn't just go and do it anyway. And get away with it.'

I dutifully thought.

'Nope.'

'There you go.' Zareen quirked a brow at me.

I took this to mean, *Go do your Ves thing.*

She was right. I was going, one way or another. I'd rather do it with Milady's official sanction than without, but whatever.

I felt better.

'Hey, maybe we can take you along, too,' I offered, brightly smiling. My idea of gratitude. Not everybody appreciates it.

'Seems unlikely there'd be cause,' was her only reply. And she had reason. I mean, Zareen's particular talents might more rightly be termed *peculiar*.

That said.

Famous last words.

I worked my magic on Ophelia next (the charismatic kind, not the enchantment kind. The former might not succeed, but the latter would get me squashed like a bug).

I found her intransigent.

'But you'd be wonderful,' I protested, smiling in the face of a flint-eyed glare from my usually mild-mannered tutor. 'Think how much everyone would learn!'

I'd hopped through to the Merlin cottage via the personal gateway I have in my room. Ophelia made it for me, even drew a pretty silver star to mark the location. I chose to interpret that as a mark of special favour, not merely a practicality. I mean, she could have just drawn a big, black 'X'.

I found her engaged in study, as was common. That, or she was indulging in her secret(ish) passion for Georgette Heyer novels. She was tucked up in an overstuffed armchair and I couldn't see much of the book she was clutching, except that it looked rather ragged.

Having swept in like the whirlwind I am, I'd started arguing for the lecture immediately. 'Ophelia! Zareen and I had the *best* idea.'

It all went downhill from there, but, to be fair, that was according to plan.

'I am no lecturer.' Ophelia shut her book with a decisive, and disapproving, *snap.* I caught a glimpse of the title before she hid it away. *The Talisman Ring.* 'And,' she added, somewhat ruining the impact of a statement so sternly intoned, 'Merlin's arts are not for everyone.'

'True,' I agreed. 'Just for you. And me.'

She looked at me with an expression I tried not to interpret as second thoughts on that latter point.

'I understand,' I said hastily. 'Wouldn't dream of pushing.'

She waited, sceptical.

I suppose, after a couple of months, she's getting used to me.

'Can I have next Tuesday off?' I said, possibly rushing my fence a bit. 'And maybe the one after that?'

She blinked, and her hauteur deepened. 'For what purpose?'

'There's an important assignment I need to be involved with. Might take a week or two.'

'Oh. Of course.'

It was my turn for a surprised silence. 'Really?'

'Certainly. I am not so stern a task-master as all that, I hope. There is time.'

'Oh. Well. Thank you.'

She studied me. 'Your first proposal was a deliberate attempt to unsettle me so I would agree more readily to your second.'

I opened my mouth, hoping some glib defence would spring easily to my lips.

It didn't.

'You needn't have gone to such lengths. While the prospect of your temporary absence seems trivial in comparison with the horrible prospect of my performing lectures for the benefit of a hundred reluctant students, I would have agreed anyway.'

'I see that now,' I said in a small voice.

'Consequently, the complimentary nerve-shattering was unnecessary.'

I mulled that over. She was right. Why had I imagined I'd have to manoeuvre her into it? It was Milady who arranged my schedule — and held decided opinions about it, at that.

Perhaps I'd got so used to dealing with my mother, I'd forgotten that not everybody said 'no' as a matter of course.

'I apologise,' I said. 'Another time I will simply enquire.'

To my relief, she began to look more amused than affronted. 'I perceive that few people ever really refuse you anything,' she said, curiously echoing what Zareen had said earlier in the day.

I began to wonder if I was viewed as a spoiled, wheedling child by the Society at large, and decided not to pursue the subject any further.

'Just my mother,' I offered. 'It doesn't stick.'

THREE DAYS PASSED; DAYS in which Indira remained close-mouthed about the regulator, Milady did not summon me for a mission briefing, and Jay did not return.

By Friday my mood had gone from *grey and drizzly* to *storm warnings, take cover.*

By Sunday I was out in the unicorn grove, sulking. I'd love to say something more flattering, like, *acknowledging my feelings and engaging in judicious self-care,* but I was sulking. The ears were down, the tail was drooping, I was eating *grass*, for goodness' sake.

So when Jay suddenly appeared, the sun came out again in my sad little world and I went to meet him all a-frisk.

'And there she is,' said Jay, striding into the heart of Addie's grove and smiling. I think. I may not have mentioned this, but human expression can look a little different when you aren't presently being one. The stretching of Jay's face in sideways directions, the baring of the teeth; these registered with me as *good* and *odd* in about equal measure.

I gambolled coquettishly towards him, tossing my mane. If there was a just goddess in attendance then there ought to have been an opportune gust of wind at just that moment, blowing back my hair, and a ray of sunlight like a star gleaming at the tip of my horn.

There probably wasn't.

There definitely wasn't, for Jay's smile disappeared and he took a step back. 'Wait. Are you okay? What are you doing? Is there something wrong with your legs?'

I suppose unicorn mannerisms are no more easily comprehensible to a human. So much for my joyous prance of welcome. I sniffed and shoved him with my nose.

He grinned and stroked it for me. 'Do you fancy coming out, or should I come back next week?'

I answered this question by setting off for the exit at a brisk trot. Jay had to run to keep up with me, which he did with enviable grace. He looked good. Like always. Dressed in jeans and his beloved black jacket. Slightly tousled hair, but the look suited him.

'Great, so,' Jay said, keeping pace with me without apparent effort, 'what do we know about Silvessen?

What? I shook my head. Nothing. What are you talking about.

'That's what I thought. Which makes it the perfect choice, I suppose, because if even you don't know any thing about it then probably no one's very attached to the place. Means we can do some pretty thorough testing and just, see what the results are, no great pressure. I— uh, Ves? Wait?'

This speech confused me to the point of frustration, for I had no idea what he was talking about and no way of saying so.

So, I took off for the exit at a dead gallop, leaving Jay to high-tail it after me. So to speak. *Oh*, what kind of a unicorn would he be, if he could be one? Dark and sexy. No question.

Having wound my way through the maze of silver-leaved bushes, roses that shouldn't have been in flower, draping willow trees and other faerie paraphernalia with practised ease, I raced over the threshold of Addie's grove and collapsed in a Ves-shaped heap on the other side of it.

Jay took another couple of minutes to reach me, time which I spent checking that my clothing was correct (yes), arranging my disordered hair (important) and regaining my composure.

So, when Jay burst out of the grove, looking windblown and wild-eyed and, I judged, confused, I was able to say, with a certain icy cool: 'Testing? Testing *what*?'

'The, um. The regu— Milady hasn't told you?'

'No. She has not.'

Jay stopped dead. 'Oh.'

Oh indeed.

This was it, then. My request had been denied. I'd been excluded from the mission I had a unique right to be part of — even Milady had agreed that no one was better suited to the job.

And, okay, I was going to find a way to go along anyway, sneak if I had to. But, still. Everyone else thought I should be left out.

I felt like I'd been punched.

'It's... probably because of your training,' Jay offered. 'It's really important.'

'That's what Milady said, when I asked her if I could go last week.'

Jay nodded. 'It is really important,' he said again.

I felt too forlorn to reply. I wasn't even angry, just gutted. Jay was going, Indira would be going, someone from the Troll Court, most likely — maybe even Emellana Rogan, my personal hero.

And I'd be stuck at home, going deep with myself so I could understand just how much magick *and lacerated feelings* were lurking down there.

'I'm sorry, Ves,' said Jay, apparently reading some fraction of this in my face.

I nodded and turned away. Back Home, then. I had homework for Ophelia that I hadn't finished, because I was hoping I wouldn't need to for a couple of weeks. Then, on Tuesday, lessons. Or... or a rule-and-law-defying stealth pursuit of Jay's mission to Silvessen.

I was losing my enthusiasm to even try the latter — and *that* wasn't good.

Jay walked beside me in silence for a couple of minutes. I wanted to ask him how his latest assignment went, or how he was doing today, but words didn't come.

Eventually he said, 'No. You're right, it isn't okay.'

'What?'

'You should be with us.'

I tried a smile. 'Surely the law-abiding Jay isn't suggesting I break ranks and hare off after you.'

'I'm not suggesting that.'

'Oh.'

'I'm suggesting I'll refuse to go unless you're coming too.'

'Oh!'

I sneaked a sideways look at Jay. He had his mulish face on, jaw set, eyes steely.

'Jay,' I said. 'I appreciate that.'

He merely nodded, brusquely, and strode on.

This time, it was me who had to trot a bit to keep up with him.

3

'I'M NOT GOING WITHOUT Ves,' Jay duly announced, fifteen minutes later, standing in the middle of Milady's tower-top chamber with his chin high, eyes flashing rebellion.

'Certainly not,' said Milady, calmly.

The chin came down a bit. 'What?'

'Ves, you are late. I understand you were recuperating in the Grove, so I will let it pass. However—'

'Late?' I repeated, stupidly.

'A summons was sent this morning. Several, in fact.'

And I'd been sulking with the Horn Squad and had missed them all.

Oops.

'Sorry,' I gasped. 'Sorry. I'm here. And I'll go anywhere.'

'Silvessen, specifically,' said Milady.

'Great. Where's that.'

'Silvessen was a thriving village many years ago, with mention made in the Domesday Book. Scant references to it in one or two historic texts suggest it was a magickal community, home to at least one wand-wright of considerable skill. However, it has long since faded. Any source of magick it once possessed is either gone entirely, or nearly so.'

'Perfect,' I agreed, nodding.

'It also happens to be remote in location, at a little distance from other habitations. Hence, an ideal choice for a test of Orlando's prototype.'

Few inconvenient passers-by, magickal or otherwise, to interfere with whatever we'd be doing.

'Sounds great,' I said brightly.

'Perhaps.' Milady paused, then went on, without elaborating upon that slightly sinister *maybe*. 'Indira shall accompany you, as Orlando's representative. The workings of the regulator will be left to her, for she is properly trained in the operation of the device.'

'Understood.'

'Emellana Rogan has also agreed to work with us again, as the Troll Court's representative.'

I bounced a bit. I couldn't help it.

Milady paused again, for longer this time. 'And,' she finally said, 'Valerie has recommended that Zareen be included as part of your group.'

'Zar?' I echoed. 'What? Why? Not that I have the slightest objection to her being with us, but—'

'It is unusual,' Milady interrupted, 'but I find myself in agreement with Valerie's reasoning. The facts of the matter are briefly these: while little information remains about Silvessen in the historical record, there is one discernible mention which gives cause for concern. Gallimaufry has brought to our attention a short text, written by one Sumla of Witheridge in the late fifteen-hundreds, in which a village we believe to be Silvessen was described as *"a deathly place"*, and *"beyond the pale"*. It is not known why these words were used or what, precisely, they betoken. Considering that the text in question is hundreds of years old, it is likely that nothing now remains there but ruins.'

'But in case that isn't true: Zareen,' I said.

'Indeed. She assures me that she is fully recovered and ready to resume duty.'

'And what are we doing in Silvessen, precisely?'

'Your goal is to verify whether the use of the regulator can successfully alter, or indeed reverse, the predominant state of magick in a designated area. In the case of Silvessen, a successful test will see some restoration of magickal flow.'

My heart was too full to reply. Take several valued friends. Venture forth, into the ruins of a magickal community *possibly* rife with ectoplasmic activity. Deploy the hard-won regulator. Bring magick back. Save the day.

'I love my job,' I told Milady.

The air sparkled with her amusement. 'I am certainly pleased to hear it.'

An idea occurred to me. A glittering, scintillating, *brilliant* idea, and I passionately loved it from the very first moment.

But to carry it off, I'd have to be careful.

'So, considering the, um, uncertainties about Silvessen and the possibility of encountering unusual trouble,' I said. 'We'll be needing some unusual arts at our disposal, no?'

'Your *unusual* capacities may indeed prove a valuable asset, Ves, yes.'

'That's why I'm going along.'

'Besides your unique familiarity with the regulator's history and workings and, indeed, the mission's goals, yes.'

'I will do my best to be fully prepared,' I vowed.

Milady knew me well. There was a pause.

'Within reason, Ves,' she said.

'Oh, absolutely.' I beamed. 'One hundred percent within reason.'

Jay was looking at me sideways. He knew me pretty well, too.

'So!' I said, clapping my hands together. 'When do we leave?'

If you're hoping to avoid inconvenient questions, a quick subject change is always a handy tactic.

'Tomorrow morning. Please make your preparations promptly.'

'Faster than the speed of light,' I promised.

A FALSE PROMISE, OF course, despite having what they call *the best will in the world*. I did my best, though, by stepping smartly down to my room the moment Milady closed the meeting, Jay trailing along at my heels.

'Ves,' he said, in a wary tone of voice, 'what are you planning?'

'Me? Nothing.'

'You know that when people answer a question like that with the word "nothing", there's *nothing* more likely to rouse greater suspicion. You know that, right?'

'I do.'

'And you recall that I'm your faithful partner and side-kick and I've always got your back, but it does help to know what I'm dealing with? Right?'

I beamed at Jay. 'And I also know that you'd never go tell on me to Milady and ruin a plan of guaranteed genius. I do know that, right?'

'Right.'

The word was not uttered with quite the ringing confidence I was hoping for, but Jay had a point, so I took it.

'The plan,' I said, flinging open the door to my room, 'is simple. We're taking Merlin with us.'

'Okay...'

'Things could get hairy. We might need her.'

'I can't fault your logic, but Ophelia's rather retiring, are you sure she'll want to—'

'No,' I said, striding over to the silver star on the floor. 'I'm sure she *won't* want to. Which is why we aren't taking Ophelia.' I smiled seraphically at Jay. 'We're taking *me*, though, aren't we?'

I didn't give him time to reply. Another step carried me into the centre of my portal-star, and I was gone in a blink.

He didn't follow. By now, he knows better than to remonstrate with me when I've got a Brilliant Idea.

Wise man.

It not being Tuesday, I was polite enough to knock on the door of Ophelia's cottage before I interrupted her. I found her with her rough green overalls on, mixing up something sweet-smelling in an enormous pestle and mortar. Every pound of her heavy granite pestle sent up another, pungent waft of scent, and I inhaled deeply. 'That smells wonderful. What is it?'

'An emollient.' Ophelia neither elaborated nor looked up, intent upon her process. 'Hello, Ves,' she added, absently.

'Good afternoon! And I hope you've had a pleasant day.'

At that, she did look up. Perhaps it was the buoyant quality to my voice that alerted her suspicions. 'I have,' she said, eyes narrowing, 'thank you.'

'So, you know how you said that if I want something I should just enquire?'

I could see regret for these recently uttered words unfurling behind her eyes. 'I did say that.'

'I come with an enquiry.'

'So I perceive.' She set down the pestle, giving me her full attention. 'Let's hear it, then.'

'Have you heard about the new regulator?' I was never sure how much she kept up with the news at the Society. She spent so much of her time alone in her cottage, engaged in her own, solitary work.

'I have,' she nodded.

'Aha. Well, I asked for time off because a few of us are going off to test it in the field. Tomorrow.'

'Congratulations.' She smiled, a little, and I was touched. She knew me well enough to understand how excited I'd be.

'Thank you!' I beamed. 'The thing is, Milady is sending Zar with us, *just in case* we encounter Toil and Trouble. Which we very well might. Apparently there are unquiet spirits, possible undead, who even knows? So, I thought I'd better be as well equipped to deal with trouble as I can.'

'I believe I can see where we are going with this.'

'And. And! Since the whole mission is about testing a new magickal art in the field, I thought it might *also* be a nice opportunity for me to test *my* new magickal arts in the field. Two birds with one stone. Super efficient.'

Request made. I had only to shut up and wait, while Ophelia turned the idea over in her mind.

'It is too soon,' she said.

'I thought you'd say that, and you're not wrong. But really, how are we ever going to know when I'm ready unless we try things out?'

'There is some justice to that thought, yes.'

'And I will, of course, swear on my honour to remember everything you've taught me, and never to abuse my power.'

Her head tilted. She regarded me thoughtfully, and said, in a deceptively placid tone: 'How will you know what constitutes abuse?'

'Um. You've taught me a lot about ethics, and—'

'I have tried to teach you a lot about ethics. I am not sure how much of it has registered with you.'

I coughed. I do have a reputation as a rule-breaker and sometime trouble-maker, and it's not altogether unjust, now is it? But...

'You knew me by reputation when you chose me for this job,' I pointed out. 'I have to believe you'd trust me to get it right in the end. Even if I make some mistakes along the way.'

That, it seemed, was the right thing to say, for at last she nodded. 'Very well. I believe I can invest you with Merlin's magick on a temporary basis. Shall we say, one week?'

'That should be plenty. Thank you, thank you, thank you.'

She cut me off mid-gush with a raised hand, and I shut myself up. 'I will expect a full account of your doings as Merlin. An *honest* account. And I will be asking your colleagues for an appraisal of your conduct and achievements while wielding these arts.'

'That seems fair,' I said, cautiously. I knew I could rely on Jay and Zareen to soften any misdemeanours I might happen to stray into, entirely accidentally. But Indira? She was too scrupulously honest for that. And Emellana, well, she was a wild card. I couldn't tell what she would do.

I might actually have to behave myself.

Ophelia's smile returned, tinged with an amusement I might even term faintly malicious. 'It will be quite the test.'

I let out my breath in a deep sigh. 'What happens if I fail?'

Ophelia thought about that. 'I don't know,' she admitted. 'I will have to think about that if it happens.'

So I'd placed myself on trial as the up-and-coming Merlin, with criteria I would personally find difficult to stick to, and the threat of unknowable consequences if I screwed up too badly.

Excellent.

I was beginning to feel nicely alive.

4

'So, how do we do this?' I asked.

'Oh, you want to do it now?' Ophelia seemed surprised.

'I don't see why not. It'll give me a little time to get used to everything before we go.'

She nodded, and without another word she advanced on me with, apparently, serious intent.

I experienced a flicker of nerves and an odd impulse to back away. She was giving me what I'd asked for, so what was I worried about? I suppose I'd expected more argument, more discussion, more delay. But no, here she came, it was about to happen, what if I really wasn't ready—

'Oh,' I said, stupidly, because she'd bent slightly to press her lips to my forehead, and that really hadn't been what I was expecting. At all.

And that seemed to be it, for she withdrew, leaving me to process a burgeoning feeling of — disorder.

'I didn't, um. I didn't know it would make me feel *sick*,' I croaked.

Ophelia had withdrawn as far as the other side of the room. Now she came back, and put into my hands a handsome copper basin.

'I believe you will find this useful,' said she.

And, promptly, I did.

I WENT TO BED early. The sickness took a few hours to fade, and though, in the wake of it, I felt more restored to my usual self — if a bit swollen, like an overfull sponge — well, I still felt shaky. Vomiting a lot does that to a person.

Besides, I had a big day coming up, after all. A big *week*, maybe even two. Going to bed early and getting plenty of sleep would be the responsible thing to do, wouldn't it? The sort of thing an adult, capable, sensible Ves would do. So I did that. Feeling, may I tell you, rather smug about it.

I woke up abruptly, groggy and heavy-eyed, not because my alarm was singing to me but because my phone was. Loudly.

Someone was calling.

Also, someone *else* was looming over me in the nearly pitch dark and urgently shaking my shoulder.

'Sorry,' muttered Jay, stepping back. 'Ves. Stop screaming. It's me.'

'Jay, *what—*'

I didn't finish the sentence because he was shoving my phone into my hands. I looked at the lock screen.

An antique silver chocolate pot was there displayed, steam curling from its spout.

Milady calling.

A different kind of panic clutched at my heart. 'What is it? What's wrong?'

'Nothing's wrong. You're just late.'

Having uttered these words of doom, Jay retreated.

Late? For what?

'Hello, Milady,' I said into the phone, speaking very calmly despite the pounding of my heart. I was late. Late for something Milady wanted. Shit.

'I apologise for the lateness of the hour,' said she, crisply.

'It isn't... morning?' I said, fuzzily.

'It is ten minutes after midnight and you are needed downstairs.'

Typical. The one time I act like a grown-up and go to bed early, *then* I'm called for a secret meeting at midnight.

'I'll be right down,' I promised.

'We're waiting in the parlour.' She hung up, before I could ask where "the parlour" was.

I knew though, really. There's only one parlour at Home where Milady might hold a top-secret meeting at the Witching Hour.

House's Favourite Room.

I threw back the duvet and launched myself out of bed.

I MADE IT DOWNSTAIRS in record time, so it was a particularly unfortunate time to get lost in the labyrinthine corridors of House.

In the end, they sent Jay out to find me.

'Sorry,' I said, feeling flustered. Jay had been obliged to come and find me twice in fifteen minutes, and the first time I'd screamed in his face. I now stood in the midst of a crossroads, with three passages branching off from it, and I genuinely couldn't remember ever having seen such a place before in my life.

Maybe I hadn't. House has its mysterious ways.

'To be fair,' said Jay, gently taking my arm, and towing me down the left-hand fork, 'I ought to have waited.'

'What's going on?' I asked, trotting gamely beside Jay as he whisked us both past innumerable doors, all closed. 'What's the meeting about?'

'Sh,' Jay breathed. 'You'll find out in a minute.'

My, it really *was* a top-secret meeting. I obediently shut my mouth, and didn't open it again until Jay thrust open a door and led me into House's favourite room. It's a snug little chamber, dating from somewhere in the sixteen-hundreds, and unchanged since. It has the type of grandfather clock that's determined to be heard over any amount of noise, and I could clearly hear the resonant *tick-tick* of the clock over the low murmur of conversation.

Gathered around the little white tea table, deep in mugs of hot chocolate, were: Indira, Zareen and Emellana Rogan. Em had seated herself beneath a gilt-framed portrait of a troll lady in seventeenth-century court dress; the same kind I'd recently worn myself, at Mandridore. I couldn't remember ever seeing that painting before, and I wanted to ask about it, but this meeting was both secret and urgent and that'd have to wait for another time. Focus, Ves.

'Aha,' I said, taking an empty chair across from Zareen. 'Team Improbable assembles once again.'

I heard Jay snort as he took the chair next to me. 'Speak for yourself. I prefer "Team Unstoppable", thanks.'

'So far, so good,' said Zareen. 'We remain unstopped.'

'Which is the subject of this meeting,' Milady put in. 'Tangentially, at least.'

I wondered idly why we were all having this conversation in the dead of night, in a room whose existence is unknown to the majority of our esteemed colleagues.

Then I decided to be less idle about it.

'This whole thing is developing a pleasing air of *Mission Impossible*,' I observed. 'High stakes. Dream team. The toppest of top secret.'

'It has come to my attention that rumours of Orlando's work have penetrated considerably further than I had anticipated,' agreed Milady. 'And since I can no longer guarantee that such rumours will not spread beyond the borders of the Society, I have felt obliged to take further steps to preserve the secrecy of your assignment.'

In other words: a previous mission had gone rather awry when somebody (who shall remain nameless) had passed information — and other things — to Ancestria Magicka, people who ought by rights to be our allies but whose methods and goals made them soundly unpopular with us.

And since Ancestria Magicka had made it their business to interfere with us at every opportunity, Milady wasn't taking any chances with this one.

'How about the Court?' I asked, looking at Em.

'As far as is generally known, I am away consulting on a routine matter of little import,' she replied. 'Unrelated, I might add, to the Society.'

'So you arrived here in the dark of the night and snuck in?' I asked. 'That's *fantastic.*'

Em awarded me one of her faint, wry smiles. 'It was rather fun.'

'How far will this misdirection work?' Jay put in. 'After all, everyone seems to know that the regulator's ready. And then the Dream Team, as Ves put it, is immediately dispatched to parts unknown, taking Orlando's assistant along? The connection's obvious.'

'Indira has put it about that you and she are going home for a family event,' said Milady.

'She has?' Jay sounded startled, as well he might. His sister's talents may be myriad, and uniformly impressive, but talking wasn't one of them. Let alone telling glib and convincing lies to good effect.

Indira unwittingly bore out this portrait of her character by saying nothing. She only looked rather uncomfortable.

'I, meanwhile, am feeling *terrible,*' said Zareen. 'It's been a real struggle being back at work, so I am checking myself back in to rehab at the School of Weird. In fact, I left yesterday.'

'What about me?' I put in, in rather a small voice. I'd already gone through the list of believable excuses that might be spun to explain my absence from Home, and it was pretty short. If I wasn't at Home, I was out on assignment for the Society. That was it.

'You are presently engaged in a solo assignment in Leicester,' Milady informed me. 'Tracking down a rare book of possible interest to Valerie.'

'Oh, that was a kind thought. Val will enjoy lying for me.'

'In fact, you also left this evening.'

'So my continued presence at Home is shrouded in such mystery even I didn't know about it. Masterful.'

'So we're sneaking out in the morning,' Jay concluded.

'In fact,' said Milady, 'you're sneaking out in thirty-five minutes.'

'What?' I sat up. 'But we're not ready.'

'All necessary preparations have been made.'

'I'm sorry to be the problem person, but I haven't finished my preparations.' I thought I'd have time in the morning to perform the chaotic ritual I like to call "packing".

'House has packed your things,' Milady informed me.

After over a decade at the Society, I thought I was incapable of being surprised any more. It seems I was wrong.

'My clothes have been packed by a country house,' I said, just to make sure I'd got that right.

'I trust you will find everything in order.'

'I cannot say that the question of House's gender has ever troubled me much, if it can be supposed to have one,' I mused. 'But if someone's been going through my underwear drawer then I hope she's a lady.'

Milady let that pass, with her usual superb grace. Or, possibly, indifference. 'Indira has secured the regulator from Orlando,' she continued.

I had thought Indira looked unusually tense, even for her. She sat ramrod straight, with her hands clasped tightly together, and I suppose I'd attributed this to the startling news that she'd recently been obliged to lie through her teeth to her esteemed colleagues.

But, no. She had the regulator. She probably had it on her right now, for there was no way anybody was going to take that thing out of Orlando's secure workroom and then leave it lying around somewhere.

I now perceived that she had the wild-eyed look of a woman sitting on an unexploded bomb, and everything made a lot more sense.

I tried to soothe her with an encouraging smile, with the usual lack of effect.

'Can I see it?' I blurted.

Indira shook her head. 'It's secured.'

That told me exactly nothing, but okay. I wouldn't be seeing the device until we were ready to use it.

'Your instructions are as follows,' continued Milady. 'Proceed to Silvessen with all possible caution and secrecy. Please conduct a thorough appraisal of the conditions there, to be submitted via report upon your return. If you judge it safe, then Indira will deploy the regulator. You will remain long enough to observe its effects and manage any unforeseen occurrences. Once you are certain that Silvessen is hale and secure, you will remove the regulator and return Home.'

We had questions.

'Caution?' said I. 'Are we expecting some kind of threat?'

'Unforeseen occurrences?' asked Jay. 'Like what?'

'Remove the regulator?' said Em. 'Surely that would defeat the purpose.'

Milady waited until we had finished and coolly replied: 'Caution is always wise, Ves, even if the concept is somewhat alien to you.'

Fair cop.

She added, after a moment, 'And I cannot guarantee there will be no threats. The enforced secrecy of this mission is a consequence of that.'

Fair cop again. Lovely.

'Jay, if occurrences are defined as "unforeseen" then they are, by definition, a mystery. I leave it in your capable hands to manage anything that should prove troublesome, and to maximise your chances of doing so successfully I have assigned you Zareen.'

Zareen grinned. 'Don't worry,' she murmured to Jay. 'I'll look after you.'

Jay scowled. But it was a measure of his improved relationship with Zareen that he stopped there.

'As for removing the regulator,' Milady continued. 'Yes, its removal will in all likelihood reverse whatever effects its installation might produce. And if those effects are desirable, then it will be a pity to do so. But this is only a prototype, and your assignment is only to test it, and deliver a full report of its workings to Orlando's department.'

Emellana accepted this with a nod.

'Are there any other questions?' Milady waited, politely, while we all scrolled through myriad possible enquiries, and dismissed them as unworthy of her attention.

'Very well, then,' she concluded. 'I wish you all possible success, and please do exercise caution.'

We filed out, rather like a class of dismissed schoolchildren.

Only once we had put some distance between ourselves and the parlour — and, hopefully, Milady's capacity to overhear — did I own up.

'I have something to tell you,' I said, in a half-whisper.

Jay cast me a sideways look. 'Is this something to do with your abrupt and dramatic disappearance into Ophelia's cottage earlier?'

'Yes, and thank you for not haring after me.'

'I was tempted.'

'But you accepted that Ves cannot be stopped, and abandoned all pursuit as futile.'

'Exactly. So what dark deed did you commit?'

'I've, um,' I sunk my voice even further, 'I've borrowed Merlin's powers.'

Jay stopped dead, halfway down a chilly corridor, and stared at me. 'Borrowed.'

'Yes.'

'Like an old coat.'

'It fits pretty well,' I said, defensively.

'I have questions,' said Jay.

'Me too,' put in Zareen. 'Why did you do that, Ves? Do you know something we don't? Expecting something we can't handle?'

'No, and no,' I said firmly. 'It's as Milady said. We can't know what to expect. And, anyway, I wanted an opportunity to try things out in the field.'

'And *Merlin* let you.' That was Jay, solidly disbelieving.

'She did.' I flexed my fingers, which were tingling a bit with suppressed energy. 'If this is borrowing a coat, it's a supercharged dreamcoat of dizzying potential and I may be experiencing some regrets.'

Jay smirked, the weasel.

'I'm sure you will put it to good use,' said Em, bless her. How loyal.

How naïve.

'Oh no,' I said, beaming. 'I have every intention of using my powers for Evil.'

5

THIS STATEMENT DISCONCERTED INDIRA, who, of all those present, probably understood me the least.

'It's okay,' Jay reassured her. 'This is Ves. Her idea of evil is making people eat too much cake. Or turning your hair fabulous colours without telling you.'

I frowned. 'I'm sure I could think of something more diabolical than that.'

'When you do, I'd be delighted to hear about it,' said Jay. Words that would, probably, haunt him someday soon.

Indira just shook her head. I think the gesture meant "I give up trying to understand this" more than an utter rejection of my entire personal worth, but one never knows.

'I, for one, am entirely in favour of Evil Ves,' said Zareen. 'I see honorary membership of the School of Weird in your future. School tie and and everything.'

'Hey. Weird and Evil aren't the same thing, Zar. Haven't you *kept* saying that.'

'Maybe I was lying.' She shook out her green-streaked black hair, smiling with cat-like satisfaction. 'I'm Evil like that.'

'Anyway,' said Emellana, mildly intervening. 'Shall we go?'

'Onward,' I said. 'Right after I pick up our picnic from Kitchen.'

'Ves,' said Jay, with a faint sigh, 'we aren't delving into the frozen wastes, battling for survival against the uncaring elements. There'll be food.'

'You said that so beautifully.'

'And it made not the slightest difference to you, did it.'

I beamed at Jay and exited stage left, en route straight to the pantry.

I MET UP WITH the rest of Team Unstoppable outside the House. Not at the front door, obviously. That would be far too mundane. I found them skulking in the cellar, as befit such a shady mission. They were gathered around the Way-henge, Zareen leaning casually against the wall, Indira standing stock-still and tense in a corner, Emellana apparently thinking of something else entirely, and Jay pacing up and down, his phone in his hand. Everyone looked up sharply as I barrelled through the door, then relaxed when they saw it was me.

'Okay,' I panted, having done a wee bit of running on my way downstairs. 'I've got something for everyone.'

'Samosas?' said Jay.

'Check. Bhajis for Indira.'

Indira actually smiled, a bit. Nothing like food to cheer people up.

'Halva for Zareen.'

'Pistachio?'

'Of course.'

I was instantly divested of the article in question, Zareen snatching it out of my hands like a greedy child, and disappearing it with a flick of her fingers. Only a swirl of shadow remained where the halva had been, and that soon dissipated.

'And since I love you,' I added. 'I also got sholeh zard.' I handed her a Tupperware container, within which a golden and fragrant pudding lurked.

Zareen eyed me suspiciously, though she snatched the container. 'I begin to think you're buttering me up for something. What's the catch?'

'You're welcome,' I said, ignoring that. 'Em, I wasn't sure what you'd like but they told me these spiced honey pastries are popular at Court right now.'

'There are people manning the kitchen at this hour?' Emellana looked either impressed or appalled, I couldn't decide which.

'Well, there's Magnus. Nobody can persuade him to sleep.' I handed her a waxed paper bag. 'And for me, Bakewell tarts.'

'I smell something deep fried.' Jay ostentatiously sniffed the air.

'Chips for Addie. If we need her, I don't want to have to explain why I didn't bring her a picnic too.'

'Right.'

'Again.'

Jay inclined his head. 'Okay, enough dawdling, we're going.'

He said that ringingly, and with purpose, so I was puzzled when he returned to his phone and remained deedily occupied.

'I'm sure she'll wait,' I said, when a few minutes passed.

'Who?' Jay didn't even look up.

'The, uh, person you're dating.'

He did look up, then, but only to crook an eyebrow at me. My cunning attempt to find out more about Jay's mystery woman (about whom he had been notably tight-lipped) went unanswered. 'I'm finding the way,' he said.

'With the Wapp!'

'The— the what?'

'The Way-App. The Wapp. You know?'

He stared at me, and blinked.

I began to feel uncomfortable. 'What?'

Jay shook his head, a gesture remarkably similar to his sister's quarter of an hour before. I might be the death of these Patels. 'I'm wondering,' he said, putting his phone away in a pocket.

'Wondering what manner of merciful death I deserve?'

'Wondering why I didn't think of that name myself. Come on.'

I was grabbed, and firmly escorted into the henge. Zar and Em and Indira came forward, and we did a circle-of-hands thing. The Winds of the Ways began to swirl around my feet, the sense of building magick grew, and honestly the whole thing seemed very Captain Planet to this child who'd always wanted to summon the power of Heart. And there were five of us. Coincidence? I think not.

Jay's obviously the power of Wind. Emellana is Earth, with her solid-rock steadiness. Zareen is as changeable as Fire, so that leaves Water for Indira. Not a perfect fit, but

Indira's good at literally anything that doesn't require her to talk, so she'll run with it.

I was mentally casting Alban in the role of the Captain when the Winds reached screaming-pitch, and we whirled away.

'IT'S FUNNY YOU SHOULD have brought Bakewell tarts,' said Jay, once he'd got his breath back.

The comment passed me by, at first, for we emerged into a darkness so blank I felt a momentary panic. Rarely does one encounter such pitch blackness; there's usually light *somewhere*, even in the depths of night, even if it's only a faint glow. But tonight, the moon lay sulking behind a thick cloud cover and wherever we'd fetched up was obviously far from civilisation.

I collected my wits, always rather scattered after a jump through the Ways, and mustered a glowing ball of light. The ravenous darkness swallowed its soft, genteel glow, and I hastily summoned several more. Only once I had the place properly floodlit did I register Jay's remark.

'Why's that funny?'

'Because we're not far from Bakewell.'

I took a long look around.

We had appeared in the midst of a proper, *proper* henge, none of those underwhelming types where there's nothing to see save a slight mound or two. Several ancient, craggy stones over half a metre tall surrounded me in a wide circle, dark and moss-covered. Beyond them stretched a ragged moor, scrubby with grasses greenish and tawny-brown.

Bakewell. Derbyshire.

'We're in the Peak District?' said Zareen.

'We are. And this is Hordron Edge, otherwise known as the Seven Stones of Hordron.'

I shivered as he spoke, mostly because of the brisk midnight winds sweeping over the moor. Maybe a little bit with fear. I hadn't forgotten the impenetrable, blinding dark. 'That sounds suitably mystical,' I said, hoping, as I often do, to ward off fear with flippancy.

'Head west a bit and you'll hit Ladybower Tor.'

'Charming.'

'And for Zareen's interest, Cutthroat Bridge is over there.' Jay pointed off into the darkness.

Zareen grinned. 'Already I'm liking this place.'

'And Silvessen?' said Indira, all business as usual.

Em hadn't spoken. I noticed she had taken up a station by the largest of the visible stones, a great, mossy outcropping fully a metre tall. She'd placed one hand against the stone, and stood with her eyes closed.

I drifted that way. So did Jay. 'Found something?' I asked.

'Wouldn't be surprised,' Jay put in. 'They call this the Fairy Stone.'

'For good reason,' said Em, without opening her eyes. 'Whatever magic once flourished here is long, long faded, but I can feel traces of it, still.'

I hesitated, then laid a hand against the Fairy Stone myself. I'd tried this trick before, without much effect. Whatever arts Emellana (and my mother) employed to sense long-past magick, I didn't have them at my disposal.

But now I was a walking reservoir of incredibly ancient magick and things were different. The stone thrummed under my fingers, a faint, distant pulse, like the echo of a failing heartbeat.

Realisation struck. 'This was once a gate.'

'The gate to Silvessen, specifically,' said Jay. 'And our first objective is to figure out how to get through it.'

I realised he was looking at me.

So was Emellana. And Indira, and Zareen.

I felt a stab of regret. If I hadn't mentioned my borrowing of Merlin's powers, maybe I wouldn't be so thoroughly on the spot now.

I didn't have the faintest idea what to do.

'It's not like I can just, tell it to open,' I tried to explain. I could say this with authority, because I'd been trying.

'I don't know how these things work,' said Jay, shrugging.

'Me neither.' Zareen sat down with her back against the Fairy Stone, and shut her eyes. Maybe she needed a nap. It was pretty late.

Indira hovered nearby, patently deep in thought, but since she said nothing I concluded that she, too, was stumped.

I stared, pleadingly, at Em.

'The gate is long closed,' she said. 'Sealed. I would say it has been hundreds of years since it was last opened.'

'And there's no magick left here,' I put in, gloomily. It wasn't magick I was feeling in the stone; only a memory.

Jay stood with his hands in his pockets, frowning at the problem. 'Could you maybe... add some?' he said, looking at me.

'Me personally?'

He shrugged. 'You're full of lyre-magick from the Fifth Britain, and Merlin's powers to boot. If anybody can, it'd be you.'

True, that, but I couldn't say I had a great deal of control over it. Odd things happened when I touched things, sometimes, and of course there was the whole turning-into-a-unicorn thing. But the things I touched had to have some kind of magick or potential of their own before anything much would happen, and the unicorn thing only came about when I was in Addie's glade.

The Fairy Stone may have enjoyed a glittering past, but today it was dead as a dodo.

'I'm not fully trained,' I apologised. 'If there's any reviving-of-ancient-gates in my curriculum, we haven't got to it yet.'

Jay looked disappointed. I could understand why. If you've brought the embodiment of ancient British magick along on your quest, only to find that she can't open an ancient magickal gate, that's a bit of a downer, isn't it?

'Maybe... if we use the regulator.' That was Indira, so softly spoken that the wind almost whipped the words away.

'Good thought,' I allowed, cautiously. 'If it's the loss of magick that turned this gate into a dead lump of rock, maybe a revival of magick could reverse the effect.'

'But we were supposed to deploy that in Silvessen,' Jay disagreed. 'This isn't Silvessen. We're right out in the regular world, in the open. It's risky. And I'm not sure it would even work.'

'Then it will have to be Ves.' That was Emellana, sounding vaguely amused, I wasn't sure why.

Jay and Indira both looked at me, and waited.

I thought I heard a faint snore from Zareen.

'I can't do it,' I said, trying to sound calm. 'At least, not immediately. I need some time to think about it.'

And maybe call Ophelia. I didn't really want to have to call for help five minutes into our mission, that was embarrassing, but going home in defeat because we couldn't pass the first obstacle would be significantly more so.

Jay nodded, agreeably enough, but I noticed he'd begun to shiver. 'How long do you think that will take?'

'Too long for us to stand out here while I do it. I'll make you a deal.' I took my hand off the Fairy Stone, though my fingers continued to thrum faintly. 'Take us to Bakewell. Let's find rooms for the night, get some sleep. In the morning, feed me sumptuously on Bakewell tart — the proper, authentic kind — and I promise to come up with the answer.'

Jay held out both of his hands. 'All aboard the Patel bus, leaving for Bakewell in three minutes,' he announced. 'Or, close enough.'

Clinging to the prospect of sweet, almond delights to sustain me, I permitted myself to be whisked away, trying not to quail too badly under the foolhardy promise I'd made.

Idiot.

6

BAKEWELL'S POPULAR WITH TOURISTS, but not so much in October, so rooms were plentiful. Except, of course, it was stupid o'clock and tiny country towns don't have the kinds of places where you can get a room at any hour of the day or night.

So we couldn't get in to Silvessen and we couldn't get anywhere to sleep, either. So far, so disastrous.

Luckily, we had Emellana Rogan with us. If she isn't the most well-travelled woman on the planet, it has to be a close contest.

'Just a minute, then,' she said, once we'd crossed Bakewell twice looking in vain for a "rooms available" sign with lights in the windows. She gestured in the direction of the dark and barren fields, bordered with drystone walls, that ringed the raggle-taggle cluster of buildings. 'Plenty of space out there. Come on.'

I squinted, as though that might help me see farther into the darkness. 'Space?' I echoed. 'For what?'

But Em had already set off, and the rest of us had to work hard to keep up with her long stride. She led us on a forced march for some two or three minutes, then stopped in the midst of what felt to my feet like reasonably soft grass.

'We're sleeping here?' said Indira, doubtfully. 'Just on the ground?'

I could sympathise with her obvious discomfort at the idea. Indira struck me as a fastidiously neat person; rarely had I seen her with so much as a hair out of place.

Me, I was more worried about the cold.

Emellana smiled enigmatically, and gestured again, a gesture I might have termed *flamboyant* if it had been anybody but self-contained Emellana who'd made it.

The air rippled, folded itself up, and became a tent. A *glorious* tent, expansive and inviting, wrought from some airy and ethereal fabric most pleasing to mine eye.

It was warm, too, as I soon discovered. We piled inside to find blankets and pillows laid out in five bundles, and not only did the tent protect us from the freezing wind, it also seemed to be gently heated.

'Ms Rogan,' I said fervently. 'You are a queen amongst women.'

She actually laughed at that, a little. 'I consider it a fair trade for spiced honey cakes,' she informed me.

'Ooh, good point,' said Zareen, flopping down into a nest of blankets and extracting her boxes of goodies.

'So you've employed this trick before,' I surmised around a mouthful of Bakewell tart.

She inclined her head. 'Only when there is no other choice. It is rather draining.'

'Where did you learn it?' asked Indira. 'I've never come across such an art.'

Emellana finished her cakes and lay down, stuffing two pillows under her head. 'I learned it from a silk-weaver in Hangzhou.'

Indira said nothing, but her face was *hungry*, like she'd eat the whole of Hangzhou alive if doing so would procure her its secrets.

'Not yet,' said Jay, shaking his head at his sister. 'You haven't got time.'

Indira sighed in agreement, and flopped into her blankets.

'Time to sleep,' I decided. 'Big day tomorrow.'

Awfully sensible of me, wasn't it? Right up there with all that *going to bed early* I'd tried to do earlier in the evening.

But despite the delicious comfort of my blankets and pillows — almost as good as a real bed, you'd hardly know you were lying on cold, damp grass — I couldn't sleep.

My mind turned and turned upon the problem of the Fairy Stone, and the foolish promise I'd made to solve it post-haste.

Promises are dangerous things. They're only made of words, and I've been forming sentences for a while now. Too easy to make.

Keeping them is the harder part, but one rarely thinks about that while uttering grandiloquent oaths. Whatever confidence I'd felt an hour ago had disappeared somewhere.

I couldn't sleep because I didn't have time. My team were relying on me to get them into Silvessen, and whose fault was that but my own? I'd borrowed Merlin's arts for exactly this reason, and now I had to work out what to do with them.

Stifling a sigh — it wouldn't do to wake my compatriots as well as failing them — I got up again and crept out of the tent.

The clouds were clearing and the sky was a veil of stars. I stood looking up at them for some time, hoping some Muse of Magick would bless me with a flash of conveniently timed insight.

Nope.

'Fine,' I muttered, extracting my phone.

It may surprise you to learn that Ophelia owns a phone. It certainly surprised me. It isn't that she eschews modern conveniences altogether, despite the antiquity of her cottage. But she rarely bothers with them, and you know why? Because she doesn't *need* them. What do you need a fridge for if you're Merlin? She's got storage boxes that keep food chilled and they're powered by magick, not electricity. Why do you need an oven or a gas-powered stove when you can summon as much fire or heat as you like with a flick of your fingers? Ophelia's kitchen is marvellous because *she's* marvellous.

Phones, though. She might be able to communicate over long distances in magickal ways, but most of the rest of us can't. So she keeps a mobile.

In a drawer. I found it a few weeks ago, buried under a stack of papers and unrecognisable paraphernalia and clearly untouched in some time.

I took it out and quietly placed it somewhere a bit more obvious. I don't know what premonition made me do that, but I blessed my accidental forethought now as I stood in a field in Derbyshire, half-frozen and out of ideas, and hoped she'd consent to answer the thing at three in the morning.

She did. Eventually.

'Ves?' she said, crisply. Not sleep-fuddled. Probably up late working on some new, brilliant potion.

'Sorry,' I said. 'I know it's obscenely late.'

"What's the problem?'

'It's the gate into Silvessen.' I gave her a speedy precis of the situation, then waited impatiently through a rather long silence from the other end.

'It's completely dead?' she said at last.

'Seems to be. I can't find so much as a stray thread of magick in there, and I couldn't get it to accept any of mine, either.'

'It's not like a battery, Ves. You can't just recharge it.'

'So I discovered.'

She was quiet again for a time. 'It is a conundrum,' she allowed. 'The gate is inactive because Silvessen Dell is a dead enclave. Were the enclave revived, so too would the gate be, but you need to revive the gate in order to access the Dell.'

'That's about the size of it.'

'Jay cannot assist you, I collect?'

'If there is a Way-henge inside Silvessen, Jay can't find it. Probably for the same reason.'

'Hm. Then you'll have to go back a bit.'

'Back? Back where?'

'Think of Farringale and Baroness Tremayne.'

Hm. Baroness Tremayne, a troll noblewoman who'd survived the death of Farringale by centuries. In a manner of speaking. 'Between the echoes,' I said. 'I still have no idea what that means.'

'It is about memory. And dream.'

'I hate to keep being such a downer, but I have no idea what that means, either.'

'You probably do, Ves. Didn't you tell me you detected a memory of magick within the Fairy Stone?'

'Yes…'

'The Stone remembers what it once was. Somewhere, between the echoes of memory and time, there's a thread you could use.'

'All right, thank you, but how do I find it?'

'Go deeper. Remember what I've been teaching you.'

Deeper. Hm. I thanked Ophelia with as much grace as I could muster (which was less than she deserved, but what can I say? It was three in the morning, I'd hardly slept, and I was badly feeling the pressure) and hung up.

Go deeper. Right.

Sleep being out of the question, I didn't bother returning to the tent. Instead I sent a text to Jay's phone. *Meet me at the Fairy Stone,* it said. *Bring sustenance.*

Then I trudged wearily out into the grassy field. When I judged I'd put enough distance in between me and both the tent and Bakewell, I retrieved my syrinx pipes and played Addie's song.

My glorious unicorn Familiar answered promptly, as she usually does. I still had her bag of chips about me, even if they were cold by now. She didn't mind. I admired her rippling, pearly mane and gleaming silvery hide as she devoured my offering of peace and friendship, and then I was up on her back and we were galloping away.

Two or three strides in, Addie spread her beautiful wings and away we flew.

7

THE TRIP BACK TO the Fairy Stone took next to no time. My trusty unicorn friend deposited me, gently, in the midst of the Seven Stones of Hordron and began to nip listlessly at the grass thereabouts. I could understand her lack of enthusiasm. I wouldn't want to follow a meal of delicious, greasy chips with a snack of brittle, half-frozen grass, either.

I didn't dismiss her, just yet. She wasn't only my friend and occasional mount. She was my Familiar, and I was also hers, in a way. We were a team, closely bound, and if anybody could help me talk to the Fairy Stone, it would be Addie.

'Okay, so,' I told her as I approached the gate. 'Here's the problem, dear heart. This lovely stone stands between us and Silvessen, and I can't get it to talk to me. It's been asleep for a really, *really* long time, and it's probably forgotten what it was like to be a magickal portal to a thriving enclave. It's just a lump of rock now, like the rest of these. But I need it to be a gate again. Just for today. What do you think?'

Addie didn't answer, of course. I've been trying to teach her some English, but we haven't got any further than *wheehehe*, which I choose to interpret as a gleeful ejaculation, but who knows.

She lay down, though, right next to the Fairy Stone, with her gleaming hide pressed against it.

I took this as a hint, and followed suit. We formed a snuggly cluster of three — me and Addie and the moss-ridden Fairy Stone — and quiet descended.

Go deeper, Ophelia said. Between the echoes.

I shut my eyes, and sought for those faint, barely discernible echoes of long-lost magick I'd detected earlier. There they still were, right on the edge of my senses, like trying to hear somebody talking from a long way off. I focused. Maybe if I concentrated harder, I could hear the words...

They weren't words, of course. Not exactly. But the longer I sat in silent meditation, the clearer the echoes became. Fragmented wisps of memory, in scents and tastes and colours. A fragrance of cherry-blossom and almonds, and cold lakewater. A brackish taste on my tongue, and then a sweet one. A glimpse of a green freshness, sun-drenched; a star-washed night, warm and then freezing and then neither.

Memories of Silvessen, long ago. Sensations and sights and tastes that had been brought back over that threshold, by those who had once passed through it. The Fairy Stone remembered.

So did I.

I drifted, lost in memory and dream. I was ancient and boundless. I was earth and rock and rainwater. I was magick and music and the echoes of things long-lost.

And then I was grabbed and roughly shaken, possibly even a little bit *slapped*, and I opened frost-crusted eyes and blinked them blearily at the foggy shape of a someone vaguely familiar.

'Ves.' Jay bent close, looked long and deeply into my eyes. 'Ves, I need to know you're still in there. Talk to me.'

I tried, honest. I managed to make my lips move, a little, but my face was frozen solid and I couldn't even produce a croak.

Jay shook his head. He looked angry, and I wanted to apologise, even if I didn't know what for.

But then he grabbed me, hauled me close, and wrapped both arms tight around me. He was *warm*, like cuddling a radiator, and he began rubbing my arms and back, roughly, chafing my flesh.

Slowly, warmth and feeling crept back in.

'Jay,' I croaked.

He let out a sigh. 'For fuck's sake, Ves. You couldn't have waited for us?'

I stirred in his arms, but he didn't release me. That was okay. I didn't want to be released, yet. 'I thought it would take a while,' I managed to utter. 'And I couldn't sleep, so I thought...' I didn't know how to finish that sentence in a way that might satisfy an enraged Jay, so I didn't try.

I peeped over his shoulder. There was Em, standing right behind Jay and watching me with palpable concern. So were Indira and Zareen, faces etched in a slowly fading horror, and if I'd even scared *Zar* then obviously I had messed up.

'Sorry,' I muttered.

Jay sighed again. To my surprise, he grabbed my head in an ungentle grip and planted a resounding kiss on my face. 'Well,' he said, in a calmer tone. 'You've done it, so there's that.'

'Done what?' I withdrew from Jay, reluctantly, but he had pulled back, so I sort of had to.

'You mean you don't *know*?' That was Zareen, whose fear had sunk into something more like annoyance.

I hauled myself to my feet, slowly, painfully. I felt a thousand years old, and consequently was grateful for Jay's steadying grip on my arms. A glance around revealed nothing of note. 'Maybe someone could humour me, and explain.'

'This is it,' said Jay. 'We're in Silvessen.'

I took another look around. Morning had broken, as the song goes, so I could see more of the landscape than I had last night. But what I saw was a rolling landscape of moor and heath, which looked right, and there was the Fairy Stone, right where it had been last night.

It took me a moment longer to realise that the other stones weren't there.

'Oh,' I said.

Zareen laughed. 'Only you could spend all night trying to open a dead gate, fail, and then turn yourself into a new one *by accident*.'

'And then not even *realise*,' put in Indira, with unusual vehemence. She was staring at me with more than a little awe, which was odd, because I'm more used to looking at her that way. She's the star pupil around here, not me.

'I did what?' I croaked.

Jay let go of my arms, me being more or less stable by then. 'I got your message,' he began. 'Bright and early, thankfully, because if we'd been much later you'd probably have frozen to death. Or not. I mean, rocks aren't especially vulnerable to the elements, are they?'

'Rocks?'

'Rocks,' Jay repeated, grimly.

I looked pleadingly at Emellana. 'Could somebody please just tell me what happened. Use small words. I'm tired.'

'When we arrived here,' Em answered, 'we couldn't find you. Naturally we were concerned. Indira thought perhaps you had found a way into Silvessen after all, but Jay felt that you would have come back through and awaited us, were that so. Zareen grew concerned that you may have gone through and been unable to come back, which naturally increased our fears for you. Only belatedly did we notice that the Seven Stones of Hordron had increased in number.'

That filtered through. 'I turned myself into a rock,' I said.

'Not just any rock,' Jay said. 'A Fairy Stone. Because when I touched it I vanished from Hordron Edge and arrived in what I'm guessing is Silvessen. The others followed. And then we spent a solid half-hour trying to figure out how to turn you back into Ves.'

This was a lot to take in. My sleep-deprived, half-frozen and only partially thawed brain struggled to keep up. 'I have no idea,' I finally offered, that being the best explanation I could come up with.

'You don't know how you did that,' Jay clarified.

I shook my head. 'Addie was here. Maybe she turned me into a rock.'

'Doubtful. This is something to do with your Merlin powers, isn't it? Ophelia gave you an idea.'

'I did call her,' I agreed. 'She told me to look for echoes. Memories. And the Fairy Stone remembered what it once was, and I... suppose I got caught up in that.'

Jay just nodded. I suppose it wasn't worth his while to tell me what an idiot I'd been, or how close I'd come to remaining a Fairy Stone for the rest of my life. I was sufficiently alive to the horror of that idea.

'How did you revive me?' I asked.

'In the end, brute force.' Jay looked a little uncomfortable. 'Nothing else worked.'

'You slapped me?' I thought I'd felt something like that.

'No!' said Jay, horrified.

'I kicked you,' Zareen clarified.

She didn't look like she regretted it, so I patted Jay's arm. 'It's okay. I barely felt it.'

A backpack lay on the ground, not far from Jay's feet. It was a cheap canvas thing and had the look of a recent purchase about it. I noticed all this because Jay stooped, opened it up and retrieved several paper-wrapped bundles from inside it.

These he piled into my arms.

'I'm sorry,' he said, vaguely. 'I got you these.'

'You had remarkable forethought,' I replied, somewhat distracted, because the parcels smelled pungently and sweetly of almonds.

I opened one. Inside, a thick pastry case contained a filling my nose informed me was predominantly composed of almonds.

'Is this... Bakewell tart?' It smelled like it and looked like it, sort of. But not entirely. The crust was puffier than the ones I'd got from Kitchen, and the filling looked denser and squashier.

'Bakewell pudding,' Jay answered. 'Tarts are not the authentic, traditional form, or so the baker informs me.'

To my surprise, Indira handed me another paper parcel. That one contained a shortcrust concoction that looked much more familiar. 'The bakers don't seem to agree about that,' she said.

I counted. Ten. Ten Bakewell somethings. 'I shall now eat two of these,' I informed the company. 'Because rocks may be impervious to the elements, but I certainly am not. And then we'll explore.'

They're large, Bakewell puddings. You would think it would be difficult to fit two in me at once, but not when I've spent most of the night as a functional gateway to a lost magickal realm.

Having consumed enough sugar and pastry to power a rhinoceros, I felt better.

'Right, then,' I said, dusting off my hands. 'If we could—' I stopped, because while I'd been absorbed in pudding, Indira had gone right ahead without me. She was hovering about ten feet off the ground, hanging there with the grace of a dragonfly, and turning in slow circles.

The rest of our merry band was clustered beneath, looking up at her with (variously) curiosity, interest and anxiety. Maybe a little awe. Most people can't levitate like that.

'There isn't much,' Indira called down. She began to descend, very slowly, one arm extended all the way out. 'But there's something. That way. I can see rooftops.'

Jay smiled at me as I approached. 'We thought we'd better check for residents before we start,' he explained. 'Just because nothing's been reported about this place in a long time, doesn't absolutely mean that nobody lives here any more.'

'Good thinking.' I felt somewhat bemused. I'd been so focused on the pastries, I'd missed the entire conversation.

Perhaps Ophelia's lessons were paying off, far better than I'd ever imagined possible. I really had focus now.

Indira landed lightly upon the frost-tinged grass, hugging her dark coat closer around herself. She was shivering. I suppose it would be a little colder up there, right in the path of the wind. Or perhaps levitation at that level took more energy than it appeared to.

'Nothing else?' Emellana enquired.

'Not that I could see from there. Just more heath. Some wooded land, that way.' She gestured. Apparently this woodland or forest wasn't in the same direction as the buildings she'd seen.

'Let's check out those roofs you saw,' Jay decided, picking up his backpack.

'Moment,' I said, looking at Zareen. 'Zar, are you sensing anything... I don't know, *weird* out here?'

'*Weird*,' she repeated. 'You mean like, ghosts and ghouls dragged screaming from unquiet slumber and bent on our destruction?'

'Pretty much exactly like that, yep.'

'Not yet.'

I permitted myself a small sigh of relief. 'Great.'

'I'll let you know when I do.'

My relief withered and died. '*When*?'

She shrugged. 'I've got a feeling.'

'A *weird* feeling?'

'Uncanny, bordering upon eldritch.'

'Super.' I hefted my own modest bag of supplies, wishing I'd brought quite a few of Ornelle's jealously guarded magickal trinkets after all. I wasn't sure I was ready for *eldritch*.

Zareen's response to everyone's palpable discomfort was a wide grin. 'Don't worry. That's why you've got me.'

'And you are scary beyond all reason,' I agreed. 'That being the case, would you maybe like to go first?'

'Hey. You're the one wielding indescribably ancient magick of awe-inspiring power.'

'You must be thinking of Indira,' I murmured, striding forth with what I hoped was a confident step. '*She* wields magick to precise and devastating effect. *I* fumble magick, make a mess of it and occasionally luck out anyway.'

'Occasionally,' Jay said, nodding gravely. 'Yes. That coincides exactly with my general observations of your success rate.'

I lifted my chin as I stalked past him. 'Just don't blame me when this all goes spectacularly pear-shaped. I *did* try to warn you.'

8

THE VILLAGE OF SILVESSEN turned out to be a ragged cluster of wattle-and-daub dwellings of considerable antiquity. Not a one of them had been built later than the fourteenth century, I'd have wagered. They were also in states of advanced disrepair.

We wandered down the central street, once a path of packed earth and stones, now a swath of soggy mud. Empty windows gaped in begrimed facades; thatched roofs sprouted holes where the dried rushes or straw had weathered away. Some buildings had lost their roofs altogether, their thick wooden beams exposed to the wind and rain.

'All things considered,' Jay said, looking around, 'more of this is left than I'd expect.'

I saw his point. Half-ruined they may be, but if these houses were at least seven-hundred years old, and they'd been abandoned for centuries, they ought to have been rubble by now. Wattle and daub isn't the sturdiest of building materials, even if it's shored up with oak.

'Em,' I said, 'are you getting anything?'

Emellana's able to sense the traces of past magick, a skill popular with field archaeologists the world over. I suppose I am too, now, but not in the same way, and Em is still much better at it. She's had practice. Years and years of practice.

'Some preservation enchantments were in place,' she answered, standing with one broad hand palm-flat against the whitewashed wall of a tumbledown cottage. 'Long gone now, of course, but they would have kept these hous-es in decent repair for some time.'

'Until the magick died,' murmured Indira. Usually so self-possessed, she seemed unusually affected by the ruin around us, her eyes huge and sad in a face drawn in thought.

'I wonder what happened,' I mused. 'And what kinds of people lived here.' We didn't know much about Silvessen, except that it had been a magickal Dell, with a settlement, once. The proportions of the buildings suggested a taller race of being had lived here; even Emellana wouldn't have had to stoop all that much to fit through the doors. But beyond that, we knew nothing.

Emellana shook her head. 'That I cannot tell.'

Neither could I, at least not by way of a cursory exploration. I'd need time and energy to go much deeper, and I didn't have those things available just then.

'It doesn't look like anybody's still around, anyway,' Jay said. We'd reached the end of the main street, and unbroken moor stretched out before us, rain-lashed grasses and wind-ruffled heath and not much else.

'In that case, I suppose we can proceed,' I said, tentatively. I was waiting for Zareen's verdict. She'd remained quiet throughout the whole of our exploration of Silvessen Village, but she was tense, alert; ready for something. Searching for something?

'Wait,' she said, softly. She was standing close to the walls of the last house on the street, looking up at the gaping remains of thatch. She didn't elaborate, but nobody wanted to disturb her by enquiring, so silence fell.

The wind whistled as it surged down the village street, and something rattled somewhere.

I shivered.

'I think...' said Zareen. 'I think there is another house.'

'In the village? We passed some side streets, we could check—'

Zareen cut me off. 'No. Not here. It's, um.' She closed her eyes. When she opened them again, they were turning darker, blackening by the moment. 'That way.' She pointed.

Jay and Indira exchanged a glance. 'That's the direction of the forest I saw,' Indira said, and Jay nodded.

'And in that forest, there is a house...' Zareen's voice had a strange, sing-song quality to it that I *really* didn't like.

We all stared at her, but she said nothing else. When she looked at me, she hardly seemed to be seeing me.

The whites of her eyes were turning black.

'Okay, Zar.' I walked forward, slowly, until I stood about two feet in front of her, and stopped. 'Zar, that's great information, thank you, but you need to come back now.'

She blinked, and blinked again. Then her eyes focused on me, and the blackness receded a little. 'Ves. Right.' She shook herself. Her ready grin was nowhere in evidence. 'I don't suppose you've got any more halva, have you?'

Silently, I removed another plastic box from my bag and handed it over. 'That's the last of it.'

She took it, and devoured half of the contents on the spot. The familiar food seemed to ground her a little more, and the whites of her eyes came back. 'Thanks,' she said to me, and then she took off, walking fast, in the direction she'd pointed in. The same direction Indira had indicated. The place where the dark forest lay. Waiting.

I was suddenly, fervently grateful that Milady had sent Zareen with us, but of course it was no coincidence. Milady had a feel for these things. She'd proved that time and again.

'SO THAT WEIRD FEELING I was having,' said Zareen, a little later. 'It's getting worse.'

We had crossed the rolling heath of Silvessen and plunged in under the trees, and I for one was having all kinds of regrets about it.

Picture the spookiest forest your imagination can come up with. Gnarled old oak and ash trees, twisted and black. A canopy so thick and dense as to block all light, shrouding the woodland in gloom. A heavy, eerie silence, broken only by your own, increasingly tentative footfalls.

Silvessen Forest had it all going on. As we delved ever deeper into the woods, we instinctively gathered closer together into a protective knot. Nobody even needed Zareen's unique powers to detect the threatening atmosphere; it was palpable.

Worse, we were having no trouble making headway, despite the closely growing trees and dense bramble thickets. A pathway wound a meandering route deeper into the wood, a path that had no business being there; the Dell was deserted. Who had been around to use it, all these hundreds of years?

'All right, I'll be the one to say it out loud,' I finally said, albeit in a half-whisper. 'This smells like a trap.'

'No question,' Jay agreed.

'But laid by whom?' answered Emellana, and her tone was more intrigued than concerned.

She had a point. Half of me might be filled with foreboding, but the other was growing increasingly curious. Who lingered still in Silvessen Dell, and why? What were they doing in an isolated house in the depths of the creepiest forest known to man or beast?

And what did they want with us, that they had laid out a trail leading right to their door?

We trudged through wet, half-frosted earth and dead leaves for nearly half an hour, as best I could judge. Then, at last, the canopy opened up and we emerged into a wide clearing.

The house was waiting.

9

THE HOUSE WAS *WAITING*, and I don't say that lightly. A great, soaring construct of dark stone and heavy
wood, bristling with chimneys and begrimed windows,
it crouched there like a spider awaiting the approach of
dinner.

I felt watched by a hundred eyes.

Zareen halted first. And if the Scary Lady's too intim-
idated to proceed, then the rest of us sure as hell aren't
going anywhere. We stopped as a group, and stared up at
the place with collective unease.

Finally, Zareen shook her head. 'Nope,' she said. 'This is
all too obvious.'

'Too... obvious?' Jay echoed.

'Look at it.' She made a dramatic, disgusted gesture at
the terrible house. 'It could have been taken from a text-

book on haunted houses. Even the Addams Family had more subtlety than *this*.'

'You do have a point, except I'm fairly sure I'm not getting it,' I said.

'The point.' Zareen considered. 'Exactly. What is the point of it? I'd say it's being operated by people who'd like to be left alone, and we're supposed to be too scared to go in. But then all they had to do was hide. Even I might never have realised this was here.' She took a few steps forward, visibly squaring up to the house. 'Instead, they've rolled out a red carpet leading straight to the door, which means we're supposed to go in, but for no purpose we're likely to enjoy.'

A fell gust of wind swept up at her words and howled through the clearing, freezing me to my bones. I began to shiver.

'So,' I said, slowly. 'Are you saying we go in, or not?'

'I'm saying...' Zareen lifted her voice, and screamed into the wind, 'Challenge accepted, bitches!'

She went forward with the unstoppable stride of a general at the head of an invincible army (which we weren't, but I didn't feel like telling her that). The damned door swung slowly open as she approached, complete with a terrible, wrenching *groan*. There was a light behind it, but not the welcoming kind.

Zareen, unfazed, stepped over the threshold.

I'm both pleased and sorry to say that the rest of us were right behind her.

The door — or more rightly *doors*, for they were enormous double doors of iron-hinged oak — swung shut behind us, with a *boom* that echoed through the house.

Jay, behind me, tested the handles. 'Locked,' he confirmed.

'Well,' I said cheerfully. 'We're in for it now.'

'Hello?' Zareen yelled. The word echoed and echoed, the sounds taking far too long to fade.

Indira and Emellana were silent, alert, looking around. So was I.

The hallway was huge and empty. Completely empty. The dark stone walls were unplastered and unadorned, the floor of near-black oak boards was bare, and there wasn't a lick of furniture. An enormous staircase wound its way up to a higher floor, bare of carpets but lined with ornate iron-wrought banisters. Passageways opened off the hallway on either side, leading into dark places I didn't really want to go into.

I couldn't see where the light was coming from. We should have been shrouded in total darkness; there were no lamps, no sconces, no chandelier. But a strange glow came from somewhere; just enough for us to see where we were going, nowhere near enough for us to feel comfortable.

Good times.

'All right, we'll have to do this the fun way,' said Zareen, brightly, but with a brittle note to the words. I fervently hoped she was as well recovered as Milady seemed to think she was. Nothing about this house was going to be easy.

I watched as the whites of her eyes filled in with black and, shuddering, looked away. I've seen that happen a few times before. I'm getting used to it by now. Sort of.

Everyone seemed to judge it best not to rush the Scary Lady, so we waited in uneasy silence while Zareen did... whatever it is that Zareen does when her eyes turn into twin pools of fathomless shadow.

At length she said: 'Well, we've got company.'

'Figured,' said Jay tightly.

'Quite a lot of it. In fact, I'd say the whole damned village is hanging around out here.'

'Any idea why?' I put in.

'They aren't talking.'

'Hey,' I said, more loudly. 'You wanted us to come here, well, we're here. And we're not here to cause anyone any harm, but we *are* rather busy. So tell us what you want, and maybe we can make some kind of arrangement.'

Zareen sighed. 'Far as I can judge, we have a host of silent spirits and a few... ringleaders.'

'These ringleaders are controlling the others?' Emellana asked.

'I believe so. They're certainly running this little show. But they won't speak to me directly.'

A door to the left of the hallway creaked as it swung open.

'That's clear enough,' said Jay.

'Too clear,' said I. 'We're not playing this game.'

'Ves,' Zareen hissed in a whisper. 'If you think I can exorcise this many spirits then please, get your head out of the clouds.'

'So we are playing this game.'

'For now.'

Emellana sat down in the middle of the hall, which was brave of her, because the place was bone-chillingly cold and that stone floor had to be freezing. She placed both her hands palm-flat against the floor, eyes closed. I wasn't particularly surprised when she presently said: 'A lot has occurred here. Most of it would fall within the realms of Zareen's particular arts, I would judge.'

'Yes,' said Zareen tightly. 'Lots of very bad things.'

If I was parsing that correctly, Zareen and Emellana were implying that the departed inhabitants of the former village of Silvessen were still in residence in this ancient wreck of a house, but was that by their own volition or not? Were they the captives of these ringleaders Zareen spoke of, or were we dealing with a swarm of ghosts all in horrible league with one another?

Questions, questions.

I eyed the door that had opened in dreadful invitation. Whatever lurked beyond it lay sunk in impenetrable shadow.

'Okay.' I sat down in the middle of the floor and opened my bag, emptying it of one last item of special interest. The plastic wrapping crackled promisingly as I spread it open, revealing a hoard of treasure.

'Ves?' said Jay, doing his befuddled-face with the eyebrows. 'What are we doing?'

'Council of war,' I answered. 'Please, join me.'

Jay was the first to do so, proving himself a staunch sidekick once again (even if he did roll his eyes a bit on the way down). He sat cross-legged at my left elbow, shrugging his shoulders in answer to his sister's look of puzzled enquiry. Indira followed suit, and Emellana. Zareen was the last, and I didn't rush her. She was still more nearly resembling some kind of semi-undead horror than the woman I knew, and you don't hassle people fitting that description if you know what's good for you.

She sat opposite me, and stared at me with those blank black eyes.

I met them squarely.

'I hereby declare the first Semi-Recumbent Biscuit Council in session,' I announced. 'Please take a comestible.'

From the hoard of treasure I'd brought, Jay selected a custard cream. Indira chose a bourbon biscuit, Emellana a shortbread finger and Zareen a gingernut.

I grabbed a chocolate Hobnob.

Twenty seconds of quiet ingestion of sugar followed, after which the atmosphere of tension had somewhat eased.

'Right,' I proceeded. 'We have choices. Option one: we declare this entire building Someone Else's Problem and walk away.'

'The doors are locked,' Zareen reminded me.

'Yes, but Jay has that thing where he makes fathomless voids in obstacles through which a person may safely escape, and while his personal ethics are frequently against his actually using it, I believe this occasion may prove an exception. Is that the case?' I raised an eyebrow at Jay.

He actually paused to think about it; apparently something in him still felt like it would be wrong to make a hole in someone's front door for his personal convenience, even if the convenience in question consisted of escaping an eldritch horror. But he nodded. 'I could do that.'

'But then do we test the regulator or not?' Indira asked.

'If we don't,' Emellana put in, 'we will have wasted the time, and the opportunity. It won't be so easy to keep sneaking out of our respective organisations without our purpose being divined.'

'I would prefer to complete the assignment,' I agreed. 'Can we test it in the village without disturbing the residents of this house?'

'That seems unethical,' Jay argued. 'They may no longer be alive, but they are still technically in residence. Silvessen was chosen for being, supposedly, unoccupied.'

I looked at Zareen. 'And you don't think we can, um, render it unoccupied.'

'*I* sure as hell can't.' She shook her head. 'Besides, while it pains me to sound like Jay—'

'Thanks,' Jay said.

'—it's considered unethical to perform exorcisms without either the spirit's consent or clear cause, such as a direct threat to one's own personal safety or that of someone else.' She sounded like she was quoting from a health-and-safety manual, which, perhaps, she was. 'That goes triple for mass exorcisms,' she continued. 'Even if I were capable of it, we can't just vaporise all these spirits merely because they're in our way.'

'So we need their consent,' I concluded. 'Either to exorcise them, or to perform the test of the regulator while they remain in residence.'

Zareen and Jay both nodded. So did Indira.

Emellana and I remained dubious; I read doubt in her face, and she notably failed to concur with the others. No wonder. She'd spent her long lifetime travelling the world, undergoing numerous and challenging adventures in the name of magickal progress. A little problem like this wouldn't seem like much to her, and she had probably done worse than exorcise a few cantankerous (and likely dangerous) spirits in her time.

Me, I just wanted to get the job done, and I never take well to pointless obstruction.

But Jay's grasp of ethics is superb, and I trust him.

'Perhaps we can attempt a negotiation,' I suggested to Zareen. I surveyed the remains of the broken biscuit box I'd brought, through which we'd been steadily munching our way as we talked. We had several decent biscuits left, mostly intact, and even a couple of chocolate ones. 'Might they accept two custard creams, several Cadbury's chocolate fingers, some rich tea biscuits and a chocolate bourbon in exchange for leaving us to work in peace?'

'Ves,' said Zareen, 'I know this can seem like a foreign concept to you, but these people aren't friendly and we do actually have to take this seriously.'

Coming from the woman who'd once turned all the oak trees lining House's driveway upside down, just for fun, that had to mean something. 'Fair enough,' I agreed. 'What do they want?'

'That seems clear,' said Jay. 'They want us to go through that door.'

'Where we will doubtless encounter a nameless but horrifying doom.'

'Bound to.'

'All in favour?' I proposed.

Everyone glanced at the shadowy door.

Nobody raised their hand.

'Me neither,' I agreed. 'Zar, what information do you have about them?'

'Some are human,' she replied. 'Or, they were in life. Some weren't. A mixed settlement. But the ones who are running this show, they definitely aren't. Or weren't. Aren't? To be honest with you, I'm not certain all of them are even dead. Technically.'

That boded ill. The kinds of non-human beings whose day-to-day business proved relevant to the School of Weird were not good news.

'Fae?' I prompted.

'Glaistig,' she replied. 'I think. More than one.'

I searched my memory. I haven't run into a glaistig before, but as I recall from my university days, they aren't necessarily malevolent, though if you catch one in a bad mood then they can be very bad news. They're usually female, usually ghostly, and always complicated.

Judging from the signs, we were dealing with the malevolent type. Possibly vengeful.

'Still not talking?' Jay prompted.

Zareen shook her head.

It was Emellana who polished off the last biscuit, and rose to her feet. 'We appear to have two choices,' she said as she hauled herself off the floor. 'Either we find out what they want, or we leave.'

Two things nobody wanted to do.

Oh well. Life's tough.

'If anything happens to me,' I said, getting to my feet. 'Tell Addie I love her.'

With which words, I completed my dramatic exit by making straight for the beckoning door, and going through it.

Darkness swallowed me, and all sounds of my companions faded.

10

I'm NOT SURE I'VE ever felt so alone in my life. The silence was so profound, I might have been the only person on the planet, never mind in the room. The darkness was absolute, save for a faint glimmer of pale, sickly light here and there, showing me where to go. I felt frozen to the marrow of my bones, shivering as I stepped forward.

I was hoping my esteemed colleagues might follow my example and take the bull by the horns, so to speak.

Failing that, I was hoping they might choose to come with me. You know, to back me up.

But nothing broke that terrible, depthless silence, and I knew I was alone. Not even Jay had followed me.

I wasted a moment in pointless self-pity as I pictured my companions piling out of the hole Jay would shortly open in the front door, leaving me behind. Following which, they would go back to their bright, sunny lives, full of purpose and potential and loved ones, and forget me entirely.

Jay would marry the girl he'd been dating and wouldn't talk about, and produce the next generation of impossibly talented, slightly Ylanfallen children. Indira would become the head of the Hidden University by the age of twenty-five, after which she would take over the planet and rule (benignly) as Empress of Everything. Emellana would embark upon a fresh slew of exciting adventures, adding to the already living legend that she was, and Zareen... Zareen would kick George Mercer out of her life once and for all (if she hadn't already), become a stable, healthy human being, and go on to exorcise many another irate spirit or enraged poltergeist.

I, meanwhile, would be stuck in here forever, alone and unregretted, which was probably what I deserved...

A tear slid down my cheek. I'd stopped walking at some point and stood with my arms hanging down and head lowered, helpless and hopeless.

Which *really* isn't like me.

My chin came up. 'Okay,' I whispered. 'You're okay, Ves. You may not be married with kids or the Empress of Everything, but you live a life full of meaning and your hair is truly excellent. And your friends love you and would never leave you behind.' I thought for a second. That about covered everything.

The feelings of bleak hopelessness faded a little.

'Okay!' I said louder. 'Nice try, but it didn't work.'

A soft *sigh* of wind gusted past me, a hollow sound, which, by way of courtesy, brought a freezing chill with it. I began to shiver, but at least the terrible weight of my own black self-pity disappeared.

'Thank you,' I said. 'While we're talking, perhaps somebody would like to explain to me what you've done with Jay.'

A mote of light appeared before me, and spread, rippling like water. A vision shimmered there: Jay as I'd last seen him, cross-legged on the floor in the echoing hall and enjoying a custard cream. But as I watched, something changed, and I realised this wasn't quite *my* Jay. He was looking at me with an expression of such utter exasperation, one might even term it... contempt. I could practically see the thoughts passing behind his dark eyes: *What a fatuous idiot. Serving biscuits and* chatting *when there's a severe threat to deal with. I can't wait to leave this fool behind and move on to better things.*

I might have flinched a little.

I'm fairly sure Jay didn't take me very seriously when we first met. I was colourful and jaunty and fabulously dressed and I don't think Jay associated any of those things with competence or skill.

But that didn't last long.

'Still doesn't work,' I said, raising my voice. 'Where is he?'

The vision rippled, and changed. Jay was striding down a shadowy corridor, its walls painted white and streaked with something dark. A light flickered oddly ahead of him, bobbed and danced, emanating a shimmery, shivery ghost-light: some kind of will-o'-wisp. He was following in its train, eyes fixed upon it, and as I watched, a nothingness opened in the floor before him, fathomlessly black.

He walked straight into it, and disappeared.

I heard him scream.

'I doubt it,' I said, as stoutly as I could manage. The vision was more persuasive than I liked.

I was shown an alternative. Jay found a door leading outside, but when it opened, he was several floors up. He didn't seem to notice, but stepped over the threshold — and fell, screaming. I watched as he hit the hard, frosted ground and the scream abruptly cut off.

Another alternative. Jay exploring some kind of ball-room, a big, echoey chamber with a begrimed, tiled floor and a dark-painted balcony for a long-vanished orches-tra. As he stepped forward, the balcony wobbled and fell, crushing him underneath.

Another. Jay had found the house's kitchens, and was poking industriously into cobweb-ridden cupboards streaked with soot. A hellish wight appeared behind him, soundless; Jay didn't notice, so he didn't move. A shimmering cord wound around his neck, and strangled him to death.

I watched several more possible scenarios, involving an abrupt and vicious stabbing, an imbibing of poisoned beverages, and a burning alive (the latter including a particularly creative use of sound; Jay's agonised screams echoed through my ears in three-part disharmony). I neither moved nor spoke, and I didn't flinch again.

Eventually, the visions stopped.

'The torment doesn't seem to be working,' I said to the empty air. 'So you might as well skip it.'

I waited, but nothing and no one answered. Neither did the horror show start up again, though, so I considered it progress.

'Perhaps you'd like to save everybody a lot of time and energy and just tell me what you're upset about,' I continued.

Nothing. My tormentors were either unable to communicate clearly, or they were having too much fun messing with my mind to bother doing so.

I heaved a sigh.

Focus, Ves. If the glaistigs don't want to play nicely, ignore them.

My mind cleared a little as I formed the thought.

It really was *terribly* dark. Why hadn't I done something about that already?

I summoned a tiny ball of light, bright as a miniature star, and stood blinking in the sudden white glare.

I'd made it halfway down a short passage. I had immediate cause to regret my light show, for the place was in a skin-crawling state of disrepair. The walls and ceiling were probably whitewashed, once, but a thick, black mould now covered every inch. Giddy gods, what hideous spores was I imbibing with every breath?

The floor was spongy underfoot, and a short way ahead of me the wooden boards had rotted through. A dark hole yawned, ready to swallow me whole if I'd taken another step or two, so the light had been a good move after all.

I averted my eyes from the mould, and pressed on, skirting carefully around the gap in the floor.

Where was I even trying to go? Good question. I'd been lured this way, but perhaps that had only been for the sake of the torturous cinematics.

Still, the situation had to be resolved, and if mass exorcism wasn't an option, then I'd have to come up with something else.

That probably meant tracking down the ethereal inhabitants, righting their wrongs, ministering to their woes, and sending everyone away happy. Ideally.

Tricky when they won't talk.

'I'd really like to help,' I tried, marching at a smart pace towards a closed door at the end of the passage.

The door swung open, hard. It hit the wall with a sharp *crack*, and shattered, falling in splintered chunks to the floor.

Hm.

'I see that you're angry,' I observed, stepping over the mess. 'And it was probably rude of us to visit without an invitation, for which I apologise. If you'd prefer for us to leave, we will.' It cost me something to say this, for leaving without accomplishing our goals was a prospect to please nobody. Manners, though. Manners maketh man. And woman.

Nobody answered, except that the door ahead of me remained open, and the door behind me remained closed.

I took that for a polite rejection of my offer, and proceeded with some alacrity.

I was herded, by a series of unsubtle signs, around a corner, up a flight of stairs, along another passageway, up another flight of stairs, and finally into some kind of turret room right at the top of the house. Which was interesting, since I didn't remember seeing any turrets or towers on the house as we'd approached.

'Secret tower-top torture chamber,' I enthused as I stepped inside. 'Ladies, you have style.'

I was less impressed when I noticed a bone-chilling wind howling through the room, emanating from a leaded window that hung ominously open.

I peeked out. The ground was rather a long way below.

'If anybody's got any bright ideas about my leaving the building in some short, *interesting* fashion, think again,' I said, stepping well back. The vision I'd seen of Jay, opening a door in the side of the house and plummeting to his death, sailed through my mind, and again I heard him scream.

Nothing happened. I wasn't herded to the window by ghostly hands, nor shoved out upon a gust of wind, so I counted my blessings.

Instead, a door opened. Not the one I'd come through. I hadn't even seen it, for it was thick with strange, silvery mould and indistinguishable from the walls.

Jay stood on the threshold.

'Ves,' he said, in some relief, and rushed forward.

I tried to stop him, but it was too late; the door slammed behind him, and a key turned in the lock.

'As rescue efforts go, this one has suffered a setback,' I observed.

Jay was too busy checking me for injury, apparently, for he had me in some kind of a death-grip and seemed unwilling to let go.

In fact, he seemed a little upset.

'Oh,' I said, as realisation dawned. 'Let me guess. You've recently been treated to a montage of eighty-ways-to-kill-your-friendly-local-Ves.'

'Not quite that many,' he said into my shoulder, somewhat muffled. 'Twenty though. Easily twenty.'

Come to think of it, I was feeling a little rattled myself. I realised this because I was in no more of a hurry to let go of Jay than he was to release me, so we stayed that way a while.

I emerged some minutes later, very thoroughly hugged, and a little eased at heart.

'It was the screams that did it,' I sighed. 'Very realistic.'

Jay visibly shuddered. 'Right,' he said, squaring his shoulders. 'Where have we ended up?'

'A tower that shouldn't exist, though at least I arrived in a sensible fashion, that being: I climbed some stairs. How did you get here?'

'I went through a door from the dining room, which I'm pretty sure was on the ground floor. I certainly didn't climb any stairs.' He shuddered again. 'Total Miss Havisham situation down there. I don't recommend it.'

'Table laden with a maggot-ridden feast, covered in cobwebs?'

'I may need a complete decontamination when we get home.'

It was my turn to shudder. 'I was expecting to find something helpful up here, but I seem to be out of luck.' The turret room was empty, even of furniture, and nobody had manifested or tried to talk to me.

That being so, I wasn't planning to stick around.

I went to the door through which Jay had emerged, and — cringing a bit, on account of the mould — I grabbed the ancient iron key, and turned it.

Slightly to my surprise, it turned easily, and I yanked the door open. We emerged onto a narrow, winding staircase, and ventured down.

I was braced for an eyeful of rotten food and dust-ridden furniture, but the chamber at the bottom of the stairs wasn't the dining room.

'I think we've found the ballroom,' I said, stepping through a stone archway.

Jay followed me. Our footsteps rang loudly on the smooth tiled floor, echoing off the mould-silvered walls. I noticed the balcony that had, in my vision, tumbled down and squashed Jay beneath it. It looked capable of such a feat, for it sagged ominously, its encircling railings missing several spiralling wooden posts.

'Don't walk under that,' I warned Jay.

He shook his head emphatically. We trailed into the centre of the dance floor, and stopped.

A door opened in the far wall.

'Oh,' said Zareen, and came through it. 'You're still alive.'

'I haven't fallen out of a window,' I agreed. 'Or been stabbed to death, or choked, or burned alive, or poisoned, or smashed to bits beneath a falling balcony.'

Zareen grimaced. 'Or eaten by spiders.'

My eyes went very wide.

'Have you seen Indira?' Jay asked, either of me or Zareen, or perhaps both.

I shook my head. So did Zar.

'But if we aren't dead,' said Zar, 'then neither is she.'

'So I figure,' Jay agreed. 'But I'd like to be sure.'

'I haven't seen Em either,' I said, frowning. I was less worried about Ms Rogan than I was about Indira, though. There's little that can daunt the likes of Emellana and less that could do her any harm.

'Speak of the devil,' answered Jay, and he sounded *awed*, which was odd — until I turned around.

Emellana, eschewing such mundane apparatus as doors, was entering the ballroom by way of the wall. In much the same way as might a patch of mould, or a puddle of water. She *oozed*.

11

'Em?' I choked, for seldom have I beheld so unsettling a sight. All seven or eight feet of her was wobbly around the edges and... and dripping. Like slime.

She was smiling, though. I suppose that was something.

'Uhm,' said Jay. 'Zareen? Any ideas?'

'Oh, because I'm the local authority on troll-slime,' she muttered.

'You're the local authority on *weird*,' Jay hissed.

Em still hadn't said anything. Once she'd finished sliming her way through the wall, she solidified again. Sort of.

I walked over to her, admittedly with some caution. When I prodded her arm, my finger sank in up to the knuckle.

'Feels like jelly,' I reported.

'Methinks this isn't Em,' said Jay.

Zareen, her attention caught, began circling the semblance of Emellana Rogan with narrowed eyes. There was something wolf-like about her gait, predatory, as though she were a carnivore in sight of a rabbit.

'Lady and gentleman,' she said, presumably to me and Jay. 'I would strongly advise you not to show any fear.'

That's like being told, on pain of death, to *relax*. Zareen's words filled me with a terror I'd barely been aware of before, and I couldn't speak through my efforts to swallow it down again.

A glance at Jay revealed a similar struggle etched upon his face.

'Super helpful, thanks,' he said weakly.

The slime that wasn't Em appeared to have tired of us, for it/she began fading back through the wall again. I averted mine eyes. It really wasn't a pretty sight.

Neither was the vision of Indira that followed, bubbling up from the floor not far from where Jay stood. She solidified just long enough to manifest an expression of indescribable evil before dribbling away again, and vanished without trace.

Jay was definitely looking unnerved now. 'I hope this doesn't mean they're—' he began, and stopped.

'They're fine,' I said briskly. 'They're very capable people and they certainly aren't dead. Though I have to wonder how you four came to split up.' Jay had once lectured me on the adage of "never split the party", and he had a point.

'Didn't mean to,' said Jay, never taking his eyes from the spot in which Indira had appeared.

Zareen was prowling the room, staring daggers at the walls. 'Tricks,' she said. 'Whoever these jokers are, they're good.'

My reply was forestalled by a new sound, and a most unexpected one at that.

Nothing horrific, as you might imagine. Screams in the night? Terrified gibbering? The bloodthirsty howls of rabid beasts bent on our destruction? At that point, nothing along those lines would have surprised me.

What I heard instead was the delicate strains of a violin, playing a single, haunting note.

Jay's head came up.

Zareen chuckled. 'You're up, Jay,' she said.

'Hey, just because I'm a musician doesn't mean I have *any* idea what's going on here.'

'Now you know how I feel.'

'Fair.' Jay folded his arms, and stared up at the balcony.

He was right: the music was coming from up there. As we listened, the melody expanded: two violins, then three, playing together in what ought to have been delightful harmony. There was a slight wrongness to it, though, a subtle discordancy that sent me into shivers.

Three ethereal violins were, apparently, playing themselves.

The tune was a dreamy waltz, lilting and compelling; my feet began to move. So did Jay's.

'Ves,' came Zareen's voice, low and urgent, but I barely heard her. Jay swept me up in his arms and we were gone, swirling around the room in a haze of melody and magick. It seemed that the ballroom changed around me—: gone were the cobwebs and the mould and the shattered glass, away went the gloom and the decrepitude. The floor firmed beneath my feet, the walls rippled into gilded colour, and golden light blazed.

My jeans vanished in favour of an airy ballgown of purple silk, and a slight weight atop my head alerted me to the presence of a tiara.

Jay looked damned fine in a dark blue tuxedo. I beamed at him, delirious with music and romance—

'*VES!*'

Something *crashed*, and something hurt, and the dream ended.

Zareen had thrown something at me. There being a dearth of suitable missiles to hand in this draughty chamber, she'd employed one of her own shoes for the purpose: a boot, in fact, and hefty. My shoulder twinged with pain where it had connected with my flesh.

That wasn't what had caused the crash, though. The balcony had split into two pieces, only one of which remained aloft. The other lay in shattered fragments all over the parquet floor.

I noticed, sadly, that my swirly dress had turned back into jeans. Even more sadly, Jay's suit was gone, too.

'Did you do that?' I asked Zareen, pointing at the wreck of the balcony.

'No,' she said tightly. 'What the hell were you two doing?'

Jay and I exchanged an uneasy glance. What had we been doing?

'Dancing?' I offered.

'Waltzing, actually,' put in Jay.

'Lovely,' said Zareen, her voice dripping scorn. 'How about a nice foxtrot next?'

I looked up. The three violins were still up there, playing on, oblivious to the damage.

'They're compelling,' I said. 'I couldn't resist.'

Zareen rolled her eyes. 'All right, let me introduce you to Haunted Houses 101. *Which* is entry-level stuff at the School of Weird, but apparently they don't teach that at regular school.'

'Can't think why,' muttered Jay.

'First rule of Haunted Houses: *do not show fear.*' She bawled the words at us, sharp as the crack of a whip, and I jumped.

'*Fail,*' she barked, pointing at me.

'Sorry.'

'Second rule of Haunted Houses: Irresistible Compulsions must *at all costs be resisted.*'

'So... no dancing,' I concluded.

'*No dancing.* Why? Because the next Irresistible Compulsion might consist of choking your best friend to death or putting a sharp blade through your partner's entrails and we wouldn't want to do nasty things like that, *now would we?*'

I revise my previous ideas as to Zareen's probable destiny. She'll be Headmistress of the School of Weird inside of a decade, and then Giddy Gods help the students.

'No, Miss,' I said hastily. 'Sorry, Miss.'

The waltz ended, and instead of violins we were apparently getting fiddles next, for the tune they struck up was — well, irresistible. I bopped a bit, and hurriedly stopped under the force of Zareen's glare.

'What's rule three?' Jay asked.

'Get the hell out.'

'Fail,' I said.

'Fail,' she agreed. 'More fool we.' She smiled, slightly, which proved a chilling expression considering that the whites of her eyes were filling in with black again.

'Zar, what are you doing?'

'Trying something. By the way, Merlin, you're not being much help in here, I'll say that.'

Ouch.

She wasn't wrong. As the wielder of ancient and fathomlessly powerful magicks, I ought to be less pervious to ghostly suggestion, oughtn't I?

'We haven't covered the chapter on hauntings yet,' I protested.

'Doesn't matter. Make it up.'

A door opened with a *creak*, and in floated Indira.

The three of us stared at her in silence.

She stared back.

When I say "floated" I do mean that literally. She hovered several inches off the ground, and considering her youthfully lithe frame, she was looking somewhat ghostly.

That and she'd had a costume change, too. Her practical trousers-and-parka combo had gone, perhaps forever. Instead, she wore a trailing gown of ragged lace, dyed an ethereal blue.

'Nice *dress*,' I approved.

'It isn't mine.'

I looked at Jay. If anybody could tell if this was the real Indira or not, it ought to be her brother.

'Were you here earlier?' he asked.

Being Indira, she thought about the question before she answered it, examining the contours of the ballroom with a keen attention. That more than anything else convinced me she was, indeed, she. 'I don't think so,' she decided. 'Did you see me?'

'Sort of. You, um, came up out of the floor.' Jay made an expressive, bubbling-up gesture with his hands.

Indira's eyebrows climbed. 'No. I certainly didn't do… that.'

Jay perceptibly relaxed. 'Far too messy,' he agreed, grinning at her. 'Where were you?'

'The kitchen.'

'With the candlestick? Or the revolver.'

'The rope, Colonel Mustard.'

'I don't know, I'm in more of a Professor Plum mood.'

I lost track of what happened next. Zareen's comment rankled, particularly since she was right. I should be using those Merlin skills I'd so cleverly persuaded out of Ophelia, or what were they even for?

I didn't know what to do, but so what. Make it up.

I was good at that.

What would Ophelia tell me to do?

Go deep.

All right, then. Look past the surface and what do I find beneath?

For one: remarkably lively house. I'm used to unusually animated architecture, so doors opening and closing by themselves, or transporting people to unexpected places, doesn't register with me as strange. But it *is* strange. There's nothing in mere bricks and mortar that can account for that, even with magick.

That's because this level of animation requires some semblance of sentience. You don't get that with a brick.

So there was a mind in there. Possibly several.

Now, it might be that the glaistigs Zareen mentioned were operating the house, too.

Or it might be that some other entity entirely was involved.

Either way, I was growing tired of waiting for them to show themselves.

I sat down, and laid one palm against the floor, the other against the wall. I closed my eyes, tuning out the sounds of Zareen, Indira and Jay debating a suitable next move, and listened.

It's not easy to listen deeply to a house. They don't talk in the ways we're used to. Theirs is a language of creaking doors and swaying drapes; the slow mesmerism of settling dust; the whispers of passage, a thunderous step, a window slamming closed in a gust of wind. The chill of rainwater on cold glass; the parched glow of summer heat on brick and stone. The dreams of ancient beams cut from long-vanished forests...

My breathing eased, and I relaxed. Really, it's quite peaceful being a house. Except for the sharp babble of voices, lancing through the silence like splinters of wood; shouting, even screaming; the shuddering *crash* as wood rots away and falls...

Oh. It had occurred to me that we'd broken in upon the glaistigs, if such they were, and without invitation. It hadn't occurred to me that we'd irritated the *house*, too.

I'm sorry.

I formed the thought in feelings, not in words, for the house comprehended nothing of our babbling tongues.

My soft bubble of regret and penitence was not rejected.

I etched a vision of our packing up and going away, emphasising *soon*.

Then I asked a question.

The answer came swiftly.

'Aha.' I stood up, opening my eyes, and turned. My concentration shattered; my tenuous link with the house vanished.

But I had what I needed.

'Zar,' I said.

She was standing near the opposite wall, her eyes entirely black, with both hands spread against the mould-ridden plaster. As I neared, I saw that the tips of her fingers had sunk into the wall.

'Not now, Ves,' she muttered. 'I'm trying to—'

She stopped, because I'd thrust out an arm and sunk my hand into the wall, right up to the wrist.

When I drew it out, I had a glaistig by the hair.

'Oops,' I said hurriedly, and let go. 'Sorry. That was ruder than I intended.'

The glaistig regarded me balefully. She was no pretty sight: thin as a wisp of wind and white as ice, her eyes dark holes gaping in her drawn face. She wore a dress almost identical to Indira's, tattered lace and ghostly blue.

'Indira, where'd you get the dress?' I called.

'I don't know,' she said, coming over. She stopped at my shoulder, and stared at our glaistig friend in some horror.

'I think you've been volunteered to join the team,' I said.

'Over my dead body.' Jay came up on my other side, arms folded.

'Over hers, more likely,' I remarked. 'Let's not do that.'

'Pity,' sighed Zareen. 'It looks damn good.'

'Top marks for style,' I agreed. 'Serious demerits for attitude.'

The glaistig fluttered, as though tossed in a strong breeze. The shattering winds of her own rage and resentment, probably. She glared.

'Leave,' she hissed.

Suddenly, she flew at me, hands outstretched, reaching for my face. Her nails were talons, cracked and bleeding.

I hadn't expected it, hadn't had time to react; I jumped back, but too slow, half fell over my own feet—

Jay caught me.

And then Zareen was there, bone-white and gaunt, jet-black and horrifying. She hissed a word, low and guttural, and the glaistig stopped dead. The apparition hung there, as though Zareen had reached out a hand and grabbed the back of her dress.

Zareen hadn't moved.

'I can't hold her forever,' she said, and the strain in her voice told me enough. 'I certainly can't hold all of them.'

'All of them?' Jay echoed, turning wildly about. A second glaistig seeped through the wall on the other side of the room, spitting fury, and a third materialised behind Indira.

The far door flew open with a *crash*, and in stalked Emellana, towing a fourth apparition in a white-knuckled grip.

'I don't like these people,' she informed us.

I wondered what visions of horror the glaistigs had used to torment Emellana. Then I took a closer look at her face, white-lipped with fury, and decided I didn't want to know.

Zareen moved. She reached out an arm towards the glaistig stalking Indira, and the apparition halted, progress arrested. But she fought, and Zareen was overtaxed.

Indira retrieved her Wand, and raised it. 'Jay,' she called.

The Patel siblings were a daunting force individually. Together, they were truly formidable.

Especially with an enraged Emellana and an angry, desperate Zareen to back them up.

We were heading for carnage.

It would be a conflict we'd probably win, but at what cost?

To us — and to the glaistigs?

After all, sometimes the enraged, homicidal ghost has legitimate grievances.

'Okay, stop,' I shouted. 'Stop. Everybody *stop*.'

They stopped. All of them.

Not because I'd asked. Because I'd *compelled*.

I'd reached out to each mind around me and *pushed*. Hard.

Jay froze, wide-eyed, staring at me. Indira's stare was appalled.

Emellana and Zareen were *angry*.

I didn't look too long at the glaistigs.

'Right,' I said hastily. 'Sorry, that was a bit more forceful than I intended. Or even, um, knew that I could pull off, and I'll try not to keep doing it, I promise. Brownie's Honour. But if we could all just calm down for a second, maybe we could talk.'

'Talk?' hissed Zareen. 'We *tried* that. Remember?'

'Yes, but attempting to hold a conversation with empty air is an exercise in futility. At least our friendly neighbourhood tormentors are here now.' I smiled brightly at the nearest glaistig. 'Hello. My name is Ves. These are my colleagues: Zareen, Jay, Indira and Emellana. We're here on assignment from the Society for the Preservation of Magickal Heritage and it's very important. I understand you're angry about something. Perhaps we can help?'

The glaistig merely snarled. 'Leave,' she hissed again.

'We will. Soon. But first we'd really appreciate permission to carry out a project in town—'

This perfectly reasonable request was answered with a furious roar, and a violent attempt to break free of my arrest.

It almost worked. They were *strong*. I couldn't hold them forever, any more than Zareen could.

'Diplomacy isn't working,' Emellana observed, in a voice of dangerous calm. 'We're wasting time.'

I thought fast. All right, I couldn't get what we needed by asking nicely, and I didn't want to beat it out of the glaistigs. Supposing we even could. That went rather against the grain.

Time to try something else.

'In that case,' I said, 'let's play a game.'

12

'A *game*?' Jay echoed. Released from my mental grip, he took a quick step back from me, shaking his head.

I felt a stab of guilt, and tried an apologetic smile. Jay didn't smile back.

Note to self, Ves: don't push your friends around. Ever.

I set the thought aside. 'A game,' I repeated. It was a gamble, I admit, but at least maybe we could all get out of this without bloodshed. Or defeat. 'Winner takes all,' I added, recklessly.

The fae often like games. I don't mean cute parlour games like Charades, or a round of Cluedo. The fae — some of them — enjoy risky games with difficult win conditions and high stakes. Beating them at any game they'd consent to play wouldn't be easy.

But they also tended to be sticklers for honour. If we could pull it off, they'd fulfil any win conditions set.

I certainly had the attention of the glaistigs, though they didn't speak. All four of them watched me with their pallid eyes, still and focused as a predator stalking defenceless prey...

Jay's face clearly said: *I hope you know what you're doing, Ves.*

I hoped so, too. But I thought of the tricks and strata-gems they'd displayed so far — *waltzing,* for heaven's sake — and thought that maybe I was on the right track.

They seemed to like playing games.

'If we win,' I went on, 'You consent to let us leave without further interference, and we're permitted to test our device in the village before we go home.'

The glaistigs didn't move.

'If you win,' I continued, 'You can do with us whatever you like.'

'Ves.' Emellana uttered my name low, warningly. Too late. I could only shrug. I'd committed us, and I'd done so with the fullest confidence that my team could beat these creatures at any conceivable game. There hadn't really been the option to talk it over first.

And it was still better than a pitched battle. Right?

'One more thing,' I added, as the glaistigs stirred. 'In any duel of honour, the challenged party gets to choose the method of combat. And since we were subjected to an unprovoked attack, and have yet to level any harm whatsoever in return, that privilege is ours.'

Zareen folded her arms. Her expression was hard, unreadable, but her attention was focused on the glaistigs. Emellana had closed up, too, hiding any further thoughts she was experiencing as to my reckless gambit.

Indira and Jay were stoic. I chose to interpret this as support.

'Not so,' said the glaistig, the chatty one. 'You trespassed.'

'Unknowingly,' I said quickly. 'We thought the house empty, because you hid yourselves from us.'

They muttered at this, and a chill wind wafted past my face. I tried not to let my deepening unease show on my face.

'You trespassed,' said the glaistig again.

'Fine. Then there shall be two events, one to be chosen by each party.'

More muttering. More rage.

I stood my ground, and waited.

'We agree,' said the glaistig at last.

'Excellent.' I beamed, trying not to imagine what they might like to do with us if we lost. 'What, then, is your choice?'

'A contest of wits,' came the answer, though it was not the same glaistig who spoke. This one stood to my right, and came drifting nearer, smiling in ominous fashion. The expression stretched her face too wide.

'Then our choice shall be a contest of physical valour,' I countered.

'Done.'

'What if it's a draw?' asked Jay. 'We each lose one and win one.'

'It won't be a draw.' I smiled with as much palpable confidence as I could muster. It couldn't be a draw. We needed to win, decisively enough to leave no doubt in the minds of these ghostly ladies that we'd bested them fair and square. Or there'd be *complications,* and I hate that.

Jay only sighed.

'Well then, shall we begin?' I directed my smile at the more talkative of the glaistigs, and waited.

She did not immediately answer. Instead, she drew herself up to her full height — rather more considerable than mine, though she was shorter than Emellana. I mean, who isn't?

Something was changing about her. She grew, steadily, less ethereal; more solid; the tattery blue gown mended its rips and rents before my eyes, and knitted itself back into the semblance of a whole, respectable garment. Her hair ceased to toss in an invisible breeze, hanging straight and black around a face no longer withered and weathered with time.

Before me stood a woman who was, unmistakeably, Yllanfalen.

The same transformation took place among her companions, and I mentally rearranged my ideas as to the nature of Silvessen. It had been an *Yllanfalen* town. Interesting.

Lucky I hadn't declared a musical contest, although we did have Jay...

'A contest of wits,' said the tall Yllanfalen. Her voice had ceased to hiss and slither; now it was ringing and clear. 'Questions, then.'

By which she meant: riddles. Inevitably. I suppressed a sigh. Fae and their riddles.

'To win, you must answer three questions to our satisfaction,' she continued. 'If you fail to answer all three, the contest is forfeit.'

'We accept,' came the answer, though for once it wasn't from me. It was Indira who spoke, and she uttered the words with every bit as much confidence as our challenger. She'd drawn herself up, too, even if her height wasn't so imposing, and stood with her chin high.

Interestingly, her dress had also mended itself.

I shot a look at Jay, containing a question. *Is she good at riddles?*

The tiny smirk I received in reply proved answer enough.

A little of my tension eased.

'Very well. Then: listen.' Our challenger looked at each of us in turn. 'Your first question. Which door leads outside?'

I opened my mouth, foolishly; the answer seemed obvious, therefore it must be anything but.

Even as I framed the thought, the single door set into the far wall became two, then three, then more… the only thing I could feel certain of was: the original door was no longer the exit.

'I suppose we can't answer that by just trying them,' I hazarded.

'The first door you touch is your chosen answer,' she replied.

'Right.'

Indira spoke up. 'Do you mean *outside* as in, out of this room? Or *outside* as in, out of the building?'

'The latter.' The words emerged snappishly; our questions were irritating our challenger.

'Your second question,' continued the glaistig. 'How did Silvessen die?'

Not a riddle, then, but a question. A mystery. Unexpected.

'Your third question: what am I thinking?'

Impossible to answer. The triumphant glint in our opponent's eyes told me she knew it, too.

I looked at Indira. Her confidence hadn't flickered.

I took heart.

'We will require time to confer,' I said.

'You have one hour.' With these words, the glaistig faded away, together with her companions.

We were left alone in the ballroom.

The silence lengthened.

'Ves,' Zareen said at last. 'I'd ask if you're sure about this, but it's a bit late, isn't it?'

'I am sure,' I said anyway. 'We've got this.'

'Might've been easier to just leave and pick a new ghost town.'

'Might have,' I agreed. 'But probably not. Couple of hours, and we'll be out of here.'

She answered only with a sour look, which I decided to interpret as concurrence.

'So,' I said, mostly to Indira. 'We have a history quest, which we like.'

'I do like history quests,' she allowed.

'To solve question two, we first need to get out of here, which means solving question one.' I smiled hopefully.

'And question three?' Emellana put in. 'That's the deal-breaker.'

'I'll handle question three,' I answered.

'How?'

'By wily means.'

'In other words, cheating,' said Jay.

'Probably. But they cheated by giving us an unanswerable question, so I'd say all's fair.'

Indira ignored the conversation. Her quick gaze was busy with the doors, all twelve of them.

'The problem,' she observed, 'is: there aren't any clues.'

True. Each door was identical to all the others: tall, wrought from dark wooden boards and set into stone frames with rounded arches. They all bore a heavy iron handle on the left side.

'Hang on,' I said. 'I'll ask.'

That won me a mystified look from more than just Indira, but we didn't have time for a long conversation about it just then. I closed my eyes, tuned out my esteemed colleagues, and focused on the house.

I tried asking directly. *Which door would take us outside?* I layered the question with visions of fresh air, mud underfoot, and the scents of grass and leaf-mould.

Either the house didn't understand me, or it didn't choose to answer. Maybe it favoured the glaistigs. They'd been living here a while, presumably.

So I listened, instead. *Go deep, Ves,* Ophelia had said, and it had worked before.

I sat down, and dived deep into the stones of the haunted house. The air curled in sluggish gusts, stale; no one had opened a window in many a year. No one had needed to.

I drifted along with it, wafting past door after door. Did I detect a fresher note somewhere? A hint of a brisk breeze streaming under the boards…

No. It wasn't going to be that simple, either.

Words pierced my awareness. Indira. *'The first door you* touch *is your choice,'* she was saying. *'Can we open them without touching them?'*

A thought. A good one.

I caught up a current of air and fashioned it into a shape of my liking: a beguiling tendril, a flexible tool in my hands.

Away drifted my tendril, and tackled the nearest door. The latch clicked open.

I caught up all the air in the room, and sent it sailing after.

The door groaned as it slowly swung open.

I did not pause to survey the effects of my efforts; I still had eleven doors to open. No easy task, this. My focus fractured after the sixth, and only by ferocious effort of will could I bring my mind back to bear.

Five more, then three…

When I opened my eyes, all twelve doors stood open, and my four companions were staring at me with some perplexity.

'How did you do that?' Emellana asked.

'I magicked it up out of thin air,' I answered. Literally true.

This meant something to Em, though. She nodded, studying my face with interest. 'You look a little different,' said she.

'I... do?' I patted my hair, looked down at my clothes. No discernible change.

'Your skin looks...'

Jay finished the sentence for her. 'Stony.'

Stony? Had I become one with the house so thoroughly that I was starting to meld with it?

Hideous thought. Also, considering what had happened with the Fairy Stone, interesting.

'It'll get better,' I said, with a confidence I had no reason to feel. Now wasn't the time either to explore that idea or to panic about it. My skin would have to remember what a Ves looks like on its own.

'Merlin stuff?' Zareen asked.

'Presumably. It's hard to tell.' Which was true. It's not like Merlin's borrowed powers had awarded me some kind of a magickal toolbox I could draw from at will. I could no longer tell *where* my magickal efforts were coming from; I was just doing different things. Sometimes.

My peculiar efforts had paid off, this time: one of the dozen doors opened onto a barren field of scrubby grass, and in the near distance, the houses of Silvessen.

'One question down,' I said, satisfied. 'Next.'

'How did Silvessen die.' Emellana shook her head. 'There's so rarely a single reason why a settlement, or a civilisation, fails. The contributing factors are usually myriad, and complex. Understanding them requires far more research than we can accomplish in an hour.'

'Another unanswerable question, then,' said Zareen. 'I think we've been tricked.'

'Probably,' I said. 'I mean, there *is* probably a trick in there somewhere.'

Silence fell. We were all looking at Indira.

'I have an idea about that,' she said. 'But nothing to suggest it might be correct. Did anyone find a library anywhere?'

Jay rolled his eyes. 'You mean while we were wandering around stewing in our own fears? No.'

'I did,' said Emellana. 'If you could call it that. Only a few volumes survive, and they're mostly rotted away.'

I thought about consulting Mauf, but discarded the idea. He'd already been consulted, and had uncovered barely anything about Silvessen. Only Sumla of Witheridge's account of it as 'a deathly place', which sounded accurate to me. Plus something about a wand-wright.

'No library,' I mused aloud. 'And no help from Mauf. How do we solve a mystery without books, team?'

'I hope that isn't just a hypothetical question,' said Jay.

'It's not. It's time for a thrilling exercise in impromptu field archaeology.' I marched towards the door showing us the view of Silvessen; it was probably only ten minutes' walk from here. Maybe less.

'We don't have time for a lot of digging,' Jay pointed out, but he did follow me.

'No, true. We'll have to rely on what we can see above ground.'

'We do have me,' Emellana remarked.

Right. Em and her capacity to sense traces of past magicks. 'You think there might be some magickal reason why Silvessen died?' I asked.

'It's a recurring theme lately.'

'True,' I allowed. She was referring to Farringale, plus a few other troll Enclaves that had been choked out by the parasitical ortherex. 'But this isn't a troll settlement.' We could be certain of that. The houses we'd passed in the village were nowhere near large enough, nor did they exhibit any recognisable features of troll architecture.

'Nonetheless, it's a possibility,' Em replied, which was true.

'Zar,' I said, as we set off across the rough, half-frozen earth between us and Silvessen. 'Let us know if you can sense any more lingering spirits somewhere out here.'

'Didn't before, but I can try.'

Indira said nothing, which wasn't unusual. I didn't press her about the idea she'd mentioned. she didn't like to hazard guesses unless they were likely to prove correct; I'd noticed this before. Perfectionism, of a sort. She'd tell us when she had evidence, and that had to be good enough.

Back in Silvessen, we gathered in a ragged knot in the middle of the main street, glancing uncertainly at the still and silent houses in their dejected, tumble-down rows. I checked the time. Twenty-two minutes had passed since the challenge began, and we'd need ten minutes to get back to the house. Less than half an hour to investigate.

'Okay,' I said. 'This is one time when it makes sense to split up.'

Jay didn't oppose me, for once. 'We'll go this way,' he announced, drawing Indira towards the tallest building in the street: a cottage of two complete storeys, the roof mostly fallen in.

Zareen set off in the opposite direction, and Emellana chose to stay where she was. Her eyes were closed. I figured she was communing with the remains of long-faded magicks, and let her be.

I picked a little house with crooked oak beams and gaping windows like lachrymose eyes, and headed for the doorway. Less than half of the door remained, hanging limply from rusted hinges. I stepped over it, and went inside.

I was immediately struck by the strangeness of the place. The remains of furniture were in evidence, albeit of a simple kind: plain oak construction, any upholstery long rotted away. A low table took pride of place in the single chamber, a pair of chairs accompanying it. One of these was pushed back, as if someone had but lately risen from it. But the quantity of dust and mould everywhere told me that couldn't be the case.

At the rear of the room, an oaken frame suggested the erstwhile presence of a simple bed. Time had reduced the mattress and blankets to a decayed and indeterminate mass; in the gloom, I could distinguish little clearly.

It took me a long moment before I realised, with a thrill of horror, that the bed's long-dead occupant was still in it.

13

'I've found a skeleton,' I said aloud. The words burst from my lips, quite loud; the product of pure surprise. Of all the things I might have expected to find in here, contorted skeletal remains definitely weren't it.

The poor soul had not enjoyed a peaceful death. That much seemed clear from the pose: twisted as though in agony, mouth agape. I could tell little else: clothes and flesh alike were long decayed, leaving only bones and dust.

I backed away, returning to the table.

The house was curiously intact, considering the state of its occupant. A pottery plate and cup stood atop the table; nothing valuable in either, but still odd. Possessions tend to be passed on when their owner dies, and considering the antiquity of this cottage and its contents, they most certainly would have found a home elsewhere. Useful objects were in short supply back in the mists of time; you couldn't just pop down to Tesco to replace a broken glass or a chipped plate. People repaired things. People reused things. So what were these still doing here?

I poked around a bit more, and found various other articles forgotten by time: a hair comb of yellowed bone, an iron pot, a set of copper syrinx pipes.

I wasn't surprised when I heard Jay calling my name.

'Let me guess,' I said, going to the door. 'You've found dead people.'

'They're just — lying there.' He looked disturbed. Agitated. He gestured, sweepingly, towards a couple of houses across the street. 'Like they lay down in bed and nobody ever came back for them.'

'They look... pained,' Indira added, coming up behind Jay. 'Like they suffered.'

I exited the cottage and took several long steps away from it, as though I could leave the terrible vision of its owner's last moments behind me. 'Same story in there. The house is full of stuff. I think you're right, Jay. No one ever did come back for them.'

I looked around for Zareen, but couldn't see her.

Em, though. She'd wandered away from her original spot, was coming towards us. Her face was drawn, ashen. I waited, sickened, for her insight.

'There isn't much left to find,' she said when she reached us. 'But there are traces of big magick.'

'Big, *bad* magick,' I guessed.

She nodded. 'I've come across something like this once before.' She stopped.

We waited, but she only frowned, troubled.

'Where?' I finally prompted.

She sighed. 'There was a village in the Rhine valley. Lassenthaler. Some kind of feud got out of hand, and... someone worked a hex.'

'A *hex*?' I stared. 'I didn't know — is that even possible?'

Her mouth twisted, half wry, half disgusted. 'They don't teach it at the Hidden University, Ves. You can see why. *This* is what a hex does.' She gestured around at the dead and rotting village of Silvessen, littered with the bones and abandoned possessions of its inhabitants.

Of course, nobody had come back for them. There'd been no one left *to* come back for them.

'A hex can be like a curse of misfortune,' Emellana continued. 'You can twist somebody until they destroy themselves, they can't help it. Or it can be like — this. A kind of plague. Far more contagious than any natural plague, because it's baked into the bricks of every house in the village. It cannot be avoided. And it kills.'

Silence followed Emellana's revelations. I didn't know what to say. My mind shied away from the enormity of what somebody had done to Silvessen.

'Why would somebody do that?' Indira finally said. Her voice was very quiet, like she felt compelled to ask the question but did not really want to think about the answer.

'Some people are abominations.' Emellana's answer was rather short, almost snapped. She didn't want to think about it, either.

I physically shook myself. 'Right. We need to move on.'

'Ves,' said Jay. 'No. We need to do something about this.'

'I *know*,' I said. 'We can't just leave all these poor people here. They should be — buried, or something. Laid to rest. And we will. But we can't do that in the next hour.'

He sighed, and cast a last, lingering look at the cottage he and Indira had explored. 'I suppose we'll never know who did it, or why.'

I wasn't so sure. My mind had wandered back to the glaistigs at the big house. Their state made a lot more sense, now. They were spirits who hadn't departed the way they were supposed to — however that worked — because they'd had too much bitterness, too much *rage*. And they had a right to that rage.

But I wondered. They *were* some of the victims of this tragedy — weren't they?

Was the perpetrator lurking up there, too?

'We should be careful,' I said.

Jay looked at me like I'd just announced an intention to quit the Society and take up a new life as a legal secretary, or possibly a call centre operative. 'Careful?' he repeated. 'You?'

I scowled. 'I do caution.'

'When?'

'Right now. We're going back up there and we'll be all kinds of cautious.'

'Yes. Going back there is the opposite of cautious. You can see how that works, right?'

Apparently my dark little thought had occurred to Jay, too. 'We're going to need their permission to bury these people,' I pointed out. 'Some of these remains probably belong to them.'

Jay gave that sigh he does when I'm right, and he's annoyed about it. 'Fine. One question to go.'

'First we need Zar—'

'Right here,' came Zareen's voice. Sort of. It had a hollow quality to it that I didn't like, and a coarseness. She didn't speak so much as she *rasped*, and something about it made my skin prickle.

I turned around with pounding heart.

I take back what I said before. I'm not getting used to the way Zareen looks when she's deep in the Stranger Arts, and I never, ever will.

'Where've you been,' I croaked.

She smiled, and I wished she wouldn't. She looked like she had just crawled out of her own grave, having been down there quite some time: skeletal and bone-pale, her dark hair wreathing her head like black smoke, eyes dark, deeply sunken hollows. Her smile was a death's head grimace.

'I've been having a chat with the fine people of Silvessen,' she said in answer.

'You found them.'

'In a manner of speaking.' The smile stretched.

I shuddered. 'Zar, I can't express how much I respect your work, but you're scary beyond all reason.'

'I know.' She smirked.

'Em thinks Silvessen was hexed.'

'She's right. Nasty stuff.'

'Okay. So we'll do something important and respectful about that soon, but for now, we've answered question two.'

'Maybe,' said Indira.

Everyone looked at her, which made her so uncomfortable she transferred her own gaze to her feet.

'Maybe?' I prompted.

'It's just that it's odd phrasing,' she informed her shoes. 'A more natural way to phrase the question might have been: "What happened to Silvessen?" Or, "What became of the town?" But she said: *"How did Silvessen die?"*

'True,' said Jay, frowning. 'You don't normally talk about a town's having *died*. You say that about a person.'

Indira nodded.

'So you think it's a trick question,' I concluded. 'She wasn't talking about the town. She was talking about a person the town was named after.'

'Somebody important,' Emellana said. 'Somebody who would live in the best house.'

'The biggest one,' I sighed. 'The really *haunted* one.'

'Social leaders are also spokespeople,' Jay suggested. 'They take the lead.'

Zareen grinned. 'Yeah. I think we've met her.'

'In that case,' I said, 'it's time to go talk to her again.'

'WE'RE READY,' I SAID, half an hour later.

We'd made it back to the ballroom with mere minutes to spare. The house hadn't wanted to let us back in; the front door was locked, and no amount of pounding upon it or jiggling the handle had made any difference. Closed.

Just when I'd begun to wonder if we'd been played — that first question hadn't been a question at all, merely a means of getting us out of the building — Indira found a side door that swung open at a touch. On the other side of it was the ballroom.

My words echoed in the empty air, settling like dust.

The air shimmered, and the glaistig appeared. The ghost of Silvessen?

'Very well,' she said. 'The first question: which door leads outside?'

I pointed at the door through which we'd entered. It still stood open, revealing the dead earth beyond.

She didn't blink. 'The second. How did Silvessen die?'

'*She* died from a hex,' I answered.

No reaction to that, either. 'The third. What am I think-ing?'

'To that question, I have several answers,' I replied. 'You're thinking that we are a cursed nuisance and you would like us to leave, but also that we make a convenient stand-in for whoever worked that hex and you'd like to torture us a bit more, too. You're thinking that the world and everyone in it owes you something for the injustice of your death, and that of your townspeople. And in all of the above points, you're right. More or less. There has been a terrible injustice done you, and we have been pretty annoying.'

No response. Silvessen, if it was she, stared at me in silence.

'Besides that,' I continued, unfazed. 'You're thinking that when I said *a contest of physical prowess* I meant a fight. With weapons. Possibly to the death. And you liked that idea, because the angry part of you really wants an excuse to hurt somebody.'

Finally: a reaction. Her features tightened, as though a frown or a grimace were suppressed. 'And was I right in that, as well?' she asked.

'I'm afraid not.'

She inclined her head, seemingly an admission of defeat. 'Well, then. In what way am I to be challenged?'

I smiled, removing my thick winter coat, and hurled it at the nearest wall. 'I challenge you,' I said, raising my voice, so the syllables echoed off the bare, mouldy walls. 'To a dance-off.'

14

THERE WAS, FOR A short time, uproar. The other three glaistigs re-materialised, hissing something at me that I couldn't catch. This was partly because my own team were raising vociferous protests at the same time.

'Ves, did you just challenge a quartet of murderous ghosts to a *dance-off*?' Jay was saying, sounding really very surprised, which was unreasonable of him; hadn't he *met* me already?

'A brilliant plan,' Emellana was saying, and I think she meant it, 'but with one grave flaw: I have no talent for dancing. At all.'

Zareen was losing it altogether. This took the form of wordless cackling, which, emanating as it did from her death's head of a face, enhanced nobody's comfort at all.

Indira just stared at me, silent and pale. When I caught her eye, she simply said: 'I can't dance.'

I smiled encouragement at my four trusty colleagues. 'I know we haven't exactly rehearsed anything, but you can trust me. Please. Will you?'

Jay knew me well enough to smell a rat. I could tell from the way his eyes narrowed when he looked at me, and *then* he folded his arms and I knew I was in trouble. 'Trust you,' he repeated.

'I won't hurt you.'

He sighed. He knew I was asking a lot more than I seemed to be. He knew, or he guessed, what I was proposing to do.

I knew he wouldn't like it.

But it was still better than an actual battle, and it was also better than fleeing the scene, defeated (supposing we were permitted to do so without further torment). I knew it. Jay knew it.

He inclined his head in a nod.

'Thank you,' I said in relief. For a moment, I'd been afraid he wouldn't back me up.

Emellana raised her brows at me. Her lips curved in a faint, wryly amused smile. 'I trust you know what you're doing,' said she.

'As usual,' I replied, 'I haven't a clue.'

She saluted me, with more than a hint of irony about it, but she was still smirking, so I decided I'd take it.

'All with me?' I asked of my team.

Zareen had stopped cackling in favour of an utterly terrifying grin. 'I get so *bored* when I'm not on assignment with you,' she said, which was a yes more than it wasn't.

That just left Indira. She still resembled a frightened doe more than the competent, powerful woman I knew her to be, and that worried me a little. But she took her cues from Jay, especially when it came to me, and if *he* was choosing to go with the crazy, Ves-flavoured flow... I watched her eyes stray from my face to his, and back again. He'd given her a reassuring smile.

'I can't dance,' she said again.

'It's okay. Doesn't matter.'

She nodded.

All right, then.

I turned back to the glaistigs. 'Out of interest,' I said, addressing their apparent leader. '*Are* you Silvessen?'

'I am.' Her ghostly visage flickered for a moment, and I saw again the Yllanfalen woman underneath. The woman she'd been in life.

'I'm sorry for what happened to your people,' I said. 'When we're done, we would like permission to carry all those left to a place of rest, employing any rites or practices you'd prefer.'

'We accept,' said Silvessen. Instantly, without so much as a moment's thought.

Had she and her companions lingered here all these years merely in want of someone to bury their remains?

How had it taken so long?

'Do you also accept our challenge?' I said.

She gave no answer, at least in words. Instead, she and her three companions joined hands and began to sway. A ripple of music began, haunting and sad, quiet at first. The violin was back on the balcony, and a pipe had joined it, though the strains I heard were complex and layered; the work of many instruments, though we saw only two. The song was palpably sad, a heartbreaking lament that tore at my soul. My face dampened with tears.

The music swelled, rising in volume until it was a blast of sound, almost physically painful. A freezing wind tore around the ballroom, centred around the four glaistigs; the whirling currents tore at my clothes, shoving me backwards.

My back hit the wall. My team were similarly afflicted; we were pinned there like a row of butterflies, flapping weakly against the insurmountable forces of the elements ranged against us. I could hear nothing over the tumult of wind and music, so whatever Jay was helpfully shouting at me was lost forever.

It wasn't a true dance-off, of course. For that we'd need rules and judges and an audience and *costumes* and there was no chance of any of that.

This was a contest of magick, expressed through music. And dance. That being so, it might be considered unwise of me to challenge a group of angry Yllanfalen; proposing to compete with *them* in a contest of musical magick is like bringing a knife to a gunfight. Oops.

That said, we had Jay. And Indira.

And me.

'*I'm going to do my brilliant and incredibly effective music-thing,*' is what I *guessed* Jay was trying to yell at me. Because he straightened after that, and began walking directly into that fell wind with all the controlled power of an action hero. He stretched out a hand to Indira, and she took it in a white-knuckled grip.

The two siblings advanced on our foes like an unstoppable tide.

The glaistigs might have opened with music, but they were dancing, too. Sort of. The swaying had turned into a fluid, free-form, interpretive-dance situation; very Kate Bush in 'Wuthering Heights'. More graceful than it sounds, despite the flailing arms and flying hair.

The roar of music began, blessedly, to diminish. Soon I could hear Jay. He was shouting something.

'*Your turn, Ves.*'

Right.

There are two main advantages to long attendance at boarding school, and those are: boredom, and extracurricular activities. There isn't much to do during evenings and weekends. It's homework or dance classes, and what kind of a person chooses homework?

Ballet was Mondays, tap on Tuesdays, jazz on Thursdays and ballroom on the weekends. I had range. And, okay, I hadn't done any of those things for some time, but my body remembered the moves.

I crossed the floor in a series of piqué turns (passable), ending with an *arabesque*. *Pirouette en dedans*, messed up my *fouetté* but never mind, onto a series of *chaînés*, *bourrée*—

'Ves,' Jay was yelling. 'You're supposed to have *shoes* for that.'

Yes, yes I was. Pointe shoes, with wooden blocks to protect the toes (or mince them, whichever happened first).

'It may surprise you to learn that pointe shoes are not typically included in my emergency travel kit.' I was a little out of breath, being more than a little out of practice, but my toes were fine, because where I lacked suitable shoes I didn't lack for suitable magick. If I could manipulate the air around me to open a bunch of doors, I could sure as hell use it to waft myself along like a dandelion seed on the wind.

The effect was charming, if I do say so myself.

My routine set, I caught Zareen up and drew her along with me. *Piqué, arabesque, pirouette en dedans, fouetté* — and Indira made three, and we were a flurry of leaves floating on the wind, Indira a being of perfect grace, Zareen a sweeping figure of intense, concentrated motion—

Jay shook his head, but resistance was futile, and he knew it.

AND THAT'S HOW WE ended up at *saut de basque sodecha*, by way of a solid series of *jetés, pirouettes à la seconde* and a pretty spectacular *cabriole*.

Maintaining sole control over a five-person dance troupe without messing it (or them) up or shredding my own sanity? No picnic. If I wasn't Merlin there's no way I could have pulled it off. And I'm pretty sure this is not what Ophelia had in mind when she handed over the keys to an ancient and indescribably powerful magickal archetype, but what can I say? Nobody died. A few pulled muscles were sustained and a bruise or two, but there was no bloodshed whatsoever and everybody walked away sane. Who can say fairer than that?

Half an hour later, we were winded and sweating and aching in more than a few places.

'Double *tour en l'air*, Ves,' Jay insisted, so I obliged, and I regretted it, but fair's fair.

Then it was Emellana's turn. She isn't built for ballet, but let me tell you, she's spectacular at flamenco.

Jay and I closed with a dazzling waltz.

'Wonderful job, everyone,' I applauded, gasping for air and smiling from ear to ear.

'Fantastic,' Zareen panted. 'Just one problem.'

'Oh?'

'We've lost our opponents.'

I turned around, searching the ballroom. No glaistigs visible to the eye. No glaistigs visible to my other senses, either.

They'd gone.

15

'I THINK THAT MEANS we won,' I said into the silence.

The silence stretched, and nobody answered me.

I raised my voice. 'If anyone would like to dispute that, feel free.'

Nothing.

I felt more uneasy than triumphant. This wasn't quite the glorious victory I'd been hoping for, and without an explanation as to where or why they had gone, we were left guessing.

Well. They'd already demonstrated a flair for creative torment. I shouldn't have been surprised.

I shrugged, and took a decisive breath. 'Votes? What do we do?'

'Proceed,' Zareen said immediately. 'We've wasted enough time.'

'Wasted? Zar, come on. We had a great time.'

She gave me a speaking look. Since she retained most of her death's head characteristics, the effect was sufficiently appalling.

'Moving on,' I said hastily. 'Anybody else?'

'I agree,' said Emellana. 'The terms of our agreement were clear, and we have fulfilled them.'

'Also, I'm hungry,' Zareen added.

'Now that you mention it, me too,' I agreed.

It came down to Jay's opinion. While he often questioned my peculiar decisions, he rarely mounted any serious objection. If he did so today, I'd listen. In fact, as a general rule, I'd do pretty much anything that registered as important with him.

I'm not sure he knows he has that power.

'I'd be happier to know for certain that they're in agreement with our proceeding with the project,' Jay said.

'Agreed,' I nodded.

'But if neither you nor Zareen can track them down, then we're out of options. They have been given more than fair opportunity to object, if they want to.'

Indira nodded along with Jay's words and seemed disinclined to venture an alternative perspective, so that was us in agreement. 'In that case, go time.' I retrieved my coat and buttoned myself back into it.

Our door still opened onto the barren fields, and we trooped out.

I left the craggy old house with a little reluctance, and not only because of the uncertainty surrounding the glaistigs' disappearance. They'd lingered there down the centuries, alone except for each other, and in a state of misery and torment. I'd wanted to offer them a way out. Zareen couldn't exorcise all four of them if they were fighting her every step of the way, but what if they agreed to it? What if they wanted to go?

Too bad. I should have mentioned it sooner; now it was too late.

The mood was subdued as we trailed back to the village of Silvessen. We were tired, we were confused, we were uneasy. But we were also victorious, and within an hour or two of completing our test and getting out of there.

We stopped in a huddle in the middle of the main street, and Indira found herself the centre of everyone's attention.

This pleased her as much as ever, for she flushed darker, and fidgeted with the buttons of her coat. 'Um, this is probably as good a place as any,' she agreed, glancing up and down the street.

'Do you need help with setting up the regulator?' I asked.

She shook her head. I watched in fascination as she tapped two fingers against the palm of her hand and produced — apparently from thin air — a tiny, shimmering device shaped like a spinning top. Argent. It glimmered with mesmerising radiance as she turned it in her fingers.

'Neat trick,' I murmured. 'Teach me some time.'

'It's just a pocket,' Indira answered.

'A pocket of... air. Apparently.'

'Something like that.'

'That's the regulator?' asked Emellana. 'All of it?'

I saw her point. The thing was tiny, even smaller than the child's toy I'd mentally compared it with. I don't know what I had expected; something bigger, certainly. More complex. Something with knobs and dials and whirling things; something *impressive,* at any rate.

'This is it,' Indira confirmed. 'Argent's really a useful substance. You don't need much of it to produce a significant effect. Orlando spent weeks condensing the size; it's more portable this way, and you don't need very much argent, which is important when you consider how little argent there is and how many Dells and Enclaves are going to need help...' She trailed off, as if realising how many words she'd strung together all in one go.

'I meant no criticism,' said Emellana in her mild way. 'I spoke out of surprise, not disapproval. It's a very clever design.'

Indira nodded. 'The rotation's useful. It creates a kind of centrifugal force which was found to have an amplifying effect. And it's quite simple to deploy.' So saying, she knelt down in the street and gently set the regulator, point first, against the mud of the long-decayed road.

After that, I felt a whisper, barely discernible, of stirring magick. The regulator began, slowly at first, to turn, silvery and rippling like water. With every rotation, the stirring of magick built and built, until it became a near palpable force.

A faint tremor ran through the earth.

Indira stood up, and took a few steps back, motioning for us to follow suit.

I scrambled backwards, needing little encouragement to clear the area. The tremors were gaining in intensity, and I began to wonder if we'd started an earthquake. These ramshackle houses wouldn't bear the force. We'd knock the whole village down.

'Indira?' That was Jay, disquieted, casting uneasy glances at the half-ruined cottages. He'd positioned himself between his sister and me, his pose wary but prepared, as if he proposed to deflect any dislodged bricks or beams from both of us at once.

'Give it a moment.' Indira, in contrast, displayed no tension at all. She stood composed, watching the regulator with a deep focus that told me she was monitoring it with far more than just her eyes.

I followed her gaze, and refocused my own attention on the regulator. I could feel it, a central force sending waves of magick surging farther and farther, like a burgeoning tide. As I watched, it began to descend into the earth, sending up a spray of mud as it disappeared from view.

Zareen stood watching with her arms folded, hunched in on upon herself. It occurred to me that she was shivering, which wasn't a good sign. Zar isn't usually sensitive to the cold. 'Is that supposed to happen?' she was asking.

'No,' said Indira. She didn't seem perturbed.

'This is a test, after all,' I observed. 'It's bound to do some unexpected things.'

The unexpected effects continued, and by that I mean they continued to get worse. The rumbling intensified, the earth shaking underfoot. Zareen fell, with an exclamation of surprise and disgust, and I toppled into Jay.

'Sorry,' I gasped.

He merely shook his head, steadying me with outstretched hands. 'Indira, maybe we should stop this,' he shouted over the noise of the tremors.

'I... can't,' she replied. 'We're committed.'

My stomach dropped. This was bad news. The cottages were mostly tumbled down already, they wouldn't bear much more of this; if we succeeded in creating a magickal resurgence at Silvessen only to reduce its structures to a pile of rubble in the process… hard to call that a success.

'Give it another minute,' shouted Indira, rather pointlessly, for we didn't seem to have any other choice.

It was possibly the longest minute of my life. I hung onto Jay while the ground heaved under our feet; Emellana abandoned her attempts to remain upright, and opted to sit down; Zareen hauled herself up, only to sink back down in disgust. Clouds of dust and ancient straw flew from the tortured roofs of Silvessen's houses, those that weren't already a collection of bare eaves and beams.

The house nearest to us creaked alarmingly, its timbers emitting a deep, tormented groan.

'We might need to run,' Jay said, and I couldn't disagree.

And then, suddenly, it was over. The ground steadied, the profound tremors fading into stillness. The ominous rumbling of brittle timbers stopped, leaving a deep, hushed silence in its wake.

I realised I was holding my breath, and let it out in a rush. 'We're okay.'

'We are.' Jay let go of me, and straightened, looking around. All the houses were still standing, as much as they'd ever been. We'd dislodged a lot of loose matter, which lay littered about the streets, but other than that, everything was—

Fine, I was about to say. But, no. Because that would be far too easy, wouldn't it?

The silence lasted only a minute or two, and then a new sound shattered the peace. A thundering *thump, thump, thump*, rhythmic and regular, like... like a drum. Several drums.

Music.

The singing began a moment later: high, ululating voices wailing words I vaguely recognised as an Yllanfalen dialect. And another sound, one I didn't immediately place.

Footsteps. Pounding footsteps marching in time to the beat of the invisible drums.

'Um,' said Zareen, looking about. 'I don't know what's going on, but I can tell you, it isn't going to be good.'

And when Zareen calls something 'not good', she tends to mean *do you have your affairs in order*?

'Skeleton,' Jay croaked.

'What?' I whirled around.

I thought that's what he said; the racket was tremendous, however melodic, and surely he couldn't have meant—

'Skeleton,' he said again, louder.

They came clambering out of the wrecked doorways of their ruined houses, stamping their fleshless feet in time to the beat of the Yllanfalen drums. So many skeletons, more than I'd imagined these houses could hold. Far more.

A phalanx of them approached from each end of the village street, marching in perfect time. Ridden with fresh, wet earth, some of them, shaking splinters of decayed wood from their shoulders, their gaping eye sockets blank as they advanced on us.

'They've raised the *entire* population of Silvessen,' Zareen choked. 'All of them.'

Every single person who'd ever lived and died in Silvessen, she meant. Not just those who'd been slain by the hex. Every single one, reaching back hundreds of years.

We were in trouble.

'They?' Emellana yelled. 'Did *they* do this, or did we?'

Giddy gods. She was right. Was it the glaistigs who'd done this, or had we somehow set this in motion ourselves with Orlando's regulator? Was it the surge of magick that had spun these poor souls out of their graves and sent them into the streets?

We'd formed a circle, the five of us, standing back-to-back in a futile attempt to defend ourselves from the advancing horde of the dead. We couldn't hope to prevail against so many, despite Zareen's presence, despite Merlin's magick. We were in *trouble.*

'This is not how I pictured this day ending,' I muttered, groping for an idea. Something. Anything. What was I Merlin for, if I couldn't deal with a mere several hundred dead people? At this rate, I wouldn't be Merlin for long.

'This is not how I pictured this *life* ending,' said Jay.

I was panicking and I knew it. My brain spun in useless circles, picking up and discarding ideas like a hyperactive kid in a sweet shop. Fire? No. I could set a bunch of them alight, but if it worked I'd take out the whole village and probably the five of us, too. If it didn't, too bad.

Air? Wind? I'd used that to good effect already, and maybe I could... what, blow them away?

Too late. Too little time. I needed strategy for a threat like this, some kind of plan, and I didn't have one. We were out of luck.

The skeleton horde was twenty feet away and closing...

I shut my eyes.

The marching footsteps stopped, all at once, as if on cue. Seconds ticked by, and nothing happened. No bony hands closed around me, tearing me to pieces. No impacts. No pain.

I opened my eyes.

They'd formed a circle around us and were standing, motionless, staring at us with those empty, black eye sockets. They'd spaced themselves out to about a metre apart, fanning out around us in even regiments.

Well, regiments wasn't the word. There was nothing martial in their posture. They didn't look like they were preparing to attack, or to defend. They looked like they were waiting. For what?

The rhythm of the pounding drums changed, and the voices fell briefly silent.

A new song was beginning.

I eyed the front ranks of skeletons.

'If I didn't know better,' I said slowly, 'I'd say that looks remarkably like... like... well, like a flash mob.'

A single, female voice began a new melody, a raw, raucous sound layered with fury. Silvessen. She was out there somewhere.

Something in the roar of drums and words must have contained a cue, because the skeletons, as one, struck a pose.

And then... they began to dance. All of them. In unison.

16

'THOSE GLAISTIGS?' I HEARD Jay mutter near my ear. 'I get the feeling they're disinclined to accept defeat.'

'Dance-off's still on,' I agreed.

'And I'd say we've been bested,' said Zareen.

I shook my head. Vehemently. 'If there's one rule I live by, it's this: never accept defeat in a dance-off against legions of the undead.'

And, hey, we tried. Jay played the Bee Gees and Donna Summer and we threw some shapes. We were a perfect disco-dancing dream team, but we were outnumbered a thousand to one and those glaistigs are *smart*. Why bother coming up with your own routines when you could just copy the other guy?

Everything we did, they did too.

I'll say this: if you've never witnessed five-thousand mostly decayed corpses perform a 'Saturday Night Fever' routine in perfect unison, you haven't lived.

And while I've rarely been more entirely thrilled in my life, I couldn't disagree when Jay finally said: 'Ves? I think we've reached a point where this could go on all night.'

Regretfully, I concurred. 'But I can't tell you how much it hurts me to be beaten at my own dance-battle game.'

We stopped dancing.

So did our opponents. Instantly.

Hmm.

'All right,' I called. 'We concede, I suppose.'

Silvessen's voice answered. 'That makes the contest a draw, does it not?'

I winced a bit as I replied. 'Yes, yes it does.'

'But I perceive that you have already availed yourselves of the boon you were to ask of us.'

I wondered how she knew that. Had they been watching us while we'd worked, or had the effects of the regulator's installation been noticeable all the way out at the haunted house?

'How about you win a prize, too?' I offered. 'Everybody wins.'

'A boon?'

'A boon.'

Zareen made a choking noise. 'Ves, you *don't* offer an enraged glaistig a carte blanche. Have I taught you nothing?'

'It's a fair deal,' I protested. 'Same deal they gave us.'

'It is fair,' Silvessen agreed, ringingly. I still couldn't see her, or her fellows. Her voice echoed out of the air, impossibly amplified.

The skeletons hadn't moved. They had frozen from the moment we had ceased to dance, as though controlled by a puppeteer who'd lost interest and wandered off.

'Nice work with the, um, villagers,' I offered, gesturing at the surrounding horde of the undead. 'Very neat.'

A long pause followed. 'True, I called them,' Silvessen finally answered. 'Some of them.'

'Some of them?'

'The regulator,' Emellana said from behind me, 'amplified the effect somewhat.'

Oh.

Silvessen hadn't summoned five-thousand dead villagers. We had.

Sort of.

'That was, um, not intentional,' I said in a smaller voice. 'Um, but you were a terrific troupe leader.'

'Was I?'

I blinked.

'I called them to the dance,' Silvessen continued. 'At first.'

'You... at first? What were they supposed to do after?'

Her silence was eloquent in ways that sent a shiver down my spine.

'Yeah,' said Zareen. 'People don't usually haul corpses out of the grave for a dance party, Ves.'

'Got it. But then... why did they...?'

Jay leaned closer to me, and spoke in a low voice. 'Notice how they copied our every move?'

'Yes.'

'And they stopped as soon as we did?'

'Yes...'

'Think about it a moment.'

My stomach dropped through the floor.

What had I been doing, besides dancing?

I'd been guiding my team's moves, that's what. Using my Merlin superpowers to shape us into an elite, perfectly synchronised dance troupe.

'The radius of effect might have been slightly larger than I intended,' I muttered.

Jay patted my shoulder. 'To be fair, this day could have turned out worse.'

Emellana agreed. 'If you're going to absently wrest control of an undead army from the hands of an enraged murder victim, there are worse things you could do with it.'

'And hey, we're in one piece,' Zareen said. 'No thanks to Silvessen.'

My face was so hot I was surprised I didn't burst into flame.

'Let's move on,' I said hurriedly. I had some things to think *quite hard* about, but that would have to wait. I'd still promised a favour to a long-dead Yllanfalen nursing an ocean of grudges, and the regulator was still out there somewhere, doing its thing. Unmonitored.

I lifted my voice. 'Your boon?' I called. 'What would you have?'

Instead of an answer, she returned with a question. 'What is it that you've done?'

She wasn't talking about the skeletons, I guessed. 'We installed a magickal device. It's new and we're testing it, but its intended effect is to reverse the process of magickal decay — or reduce the effects of magickal overflow, as appropriate — and, um, restore balance.'

The silence was longer this time.

'Did you feel a change?' Jay asked. 'An hour ago. The earth quaked, and then...'

A fair question. I didn't notice much difference, yet, but we had arrived in Silvessen approximately five minutes ago. Silvessen herself had been born and died here; the town bore her name. She had lingered down the ages through centuries of silence and decay, because... well, because she was angry.

Perhaps also because she'd loved the place.

If it changed, she would know.

'Will it work?' came her echoing voice, softer now, with a note of... hope?

'We don't know, Jay said, honest to a fault as always. 'But if it doesn't, we'll work on it until it does.'

'Then that is the boon I would ask,' said Silvessen ringingly. 'Make my town whole again.'

'You mean... magicakally?' I asked.

'In every way.'

Rebalance, repair, repopulate. Tall order.

I exchanged an uneasy glance with Jay, who shrugged. Right. Fair was fair — what choice did we have?

Especially since I'd managed to lose my own dance battle by way of the most spectacular own goal in world history.

'Could be good,' I ventured. 'Could be interesting.'

'Better hope Milady agrees,' said Zareen darkly.

Emellana was shaking with laughter. 'I think I can promise aid from the Troll Court,' she said, when she'd regained control of herself. 'Their Majesties will enjoy this story.'

'And we have Yllanfalen connections aplenty,' Jay put in.

'Right,' I nodded, ignoring Emellana's remarks with superb grace. 'You. Indira. My mum.'

'I think the Society will want to do it.' Jay smiled at me. 'I mean, what does the Society do?'

'Find things that are lost,' I replied. 'Mend things that are broken. Rescue things that need help.'

'Exactly. This project is just a little bigger than usual.'

I took a breath, feeling better. 'We have a deal,' I called. 'But it'll take time; we can't do it in a week. And we'll need to bring a lot more people down here.'

No reply came, at least not in words. But a breeze wafted past, no longer the bone-chilling cold we'd suffered since we stepped into Silvessen Dell. This was a warm, soft wind, sweet and welcoming. A good sign.

And, to my immense relief, the legions of eerily silent skeletons turned around and walked slowly away. Back, presumably, to their opened graves, there to tuck themselves back in and return to slumber.

'Okay,' I sighed, stretching my aching limbs. 'Indira. What do we still need to do before we can get out of here?'

'I need to make sure the regulator's stable,' she answered. 'Orlando said to monitor it for at least a few hours.'

'If I'm expected to go another few hours without food, I will be committing multiple murder,' Zareen informed us. 'And there aren't very many other people here, just saying.'

'Got it,' I said. 'I undertake to preserve my life and that of my friends by way of pancakes, post haste.'

'Sandwiches would be better, but I'll take pancakes if that's what you've got.'

She proceeded to stare at me expectantly, as though I might be disposed to magick up a couple of sandwiches on the spot.

Which I couldn't, of course.

Could I?

Following my mishaps in the Fifth Britain and subsequent Merlinhood, more things were possible in Heaven and Earth than I'd previously imagined.

Maybe I *could* magick up sandwiches on demand.

I tried this.

'Your face has gone funny,' Zareen said, after a while. 'Are you... doing something?'

'I'm making sandwiches.'

Zareen's brows rose. 'To make a sandwich, you take bread, tuna fish, mayonnaise and sweetcorn, and combine them to delicious effect. What *you're* doing is... no, I have no idea.'

'I'm discovering myself to be significantly less amazing than I was hoping,' I said.

'Impossible,' said Jay.

I smiled gratefully at him. 'I'm glad you feel that way, because if I can't spirit up some food on the spot then we're going to have to go out for some.'

Jay bowed. 'At your service, my lady. Lead on.'

'I'm guessing you're hungry, too.'

'Absolutely famished.'

So Indira departed for the centre of main street again, there to stand watch over the regulator. She was accompanied by Emellana, and Zareen ('Silvessen might have backed off,' Zar explained, 'but her friends are still floating around somewhere.')

Jay escorted our local Captain of Food (yours truly) to the border of the Dell, and I took us back out into the world. The real world, the one that still had life and people in it.

It felt odd, like I'd been sitting in a blank silence for hours and was suddenly thrust back into vivid life again. Jay whisked us back to Bakewell, wherein we encountered movement and colour and the sounds of blissfully ordinary daily life. In other words, people.

I wondered how Silvessen felt after centuries of nothing and decay, with only a few, equally ghostly compatriots for company.

Then I pictured how she might feel if we could turn her town back into something like Bakewell. A community again. A centre for trade and industry. A home.

A worthy mission, I decided.

'Tuna mayo for Zareen,' I said, having exited a busy bakery, laden with carrier bags. 'Cheese and tomato for you and Indira. Egg and cress, chicken salad, and sausage rolls for Em and me and anybody else who wants one.'

'A fine haul,' Jay agreed, eyeing the bags hungrily.

'Plus, custard tarts, Danishes, chocolate eclairs, Bakewell puddings and a couple of flapjacks.'

'Anything else?'

'Tea. Buckets of it.' I handed Jay a tray of drinks containers, gently steaming, which he took with the air of a man receiving a valuable and precious charge. If you want someone who'll guard the tea with his actual life and never, *ever* spill so much as a drop of it, ask Jay.

Nor did he, even during the return trip back through the Winds of the Ways. We arrived in Silvessen with cups intact, bags only mildly savaged (sorry, I couldn't help it), and plenty of good things for all.

Which was why it was a bit disconcerting to find nobody waiting for us.

'Indira!' Jay called, turning in circles (still without spilling the tea). 'Emellana!'

No one answered.

I trotted to the middle of the main street, where Indira had set down the regulator. When I laid my palm against the damp earth, I felt a pulse of magick and a faint warmth: the device was still down there and still operative.

So where were my team?

'Zareen!' I yelled, straightening again. 'Come on, you're missing the tuna mayo.'

'Here I am!' Zareen trilled. And then she came walking around the side of the same tumble-down cottage in which I'd discovered the first skeleton.

Something was wrong with her voice, I noticed in passing; she sounded sing-song and *shrill*, which was not at all like her.

Something was wrong with her walk, too. She moved stiffly and jerkily, like a clumsily operated marionette. She grinned at us, but it wasn't a smile; this was a horrifying grimace, a face-stretching pantomime of warmth and mirth that chilled me to the bottom of my soul.

If I had to guess, I'd say Zareen had gone and got herself possessed.

And if *Zar*, of all people, had ended up possessed, there wasn't much hope that Indira or Emellana could have avoided a similar fate.

We had three angry glaistigs still on the loose somewhere — and we'd left our three friends behind without us while we'd gone in search of custard tarts.

'It's official,' I sighed. 'No mission in the history of time has *ever* been this much of a disaster.'

17

'Zareen,' I said, clearly and warily, as she approached me with that odd, jerky gait. Whoever was wearing her skin hadn't had to operate a real, living body in a long time, I judged. She'd lost the knack of it. '*Zar.* Snap out of it. Please.'

There was a definite pause, or at least a slowing of the inexorable approach. Zareen was still in there somewhere. Good.

I danced back a few steps, searching my weary brain for an idea. Dealing with misbehaving spirits is Zareen's job; what are we supposed to do when *she's* the one who gets possessed?

'Jay,' I said. 'I have no idea what to do here.'

'Then it's time for some of your trademark brilliant improvisation, because neither do I.' We were backing up together, which worked fine until we ran out of street.

Zareen was closing on us, and— here came Indira and Emellana, neither of them in their right minds either.

'We need Zareen back to fix this,' I muttered to Jay. 'Can you keep the other two busy while I work on that?'

'Right.' He took off at a run.

I didn't see how he chose to carry out my somewhat peremptory request, because Zareen was getting in my face and I had more urgent problems. 'Zareen, come *on*,' I said, sharply clapping my hands. 'You're a boss and a queen and you've got this.'

She hadn't got it. I could tell from the way she tried to grab my face with her red-lacquered fingernails (rather chipped).

Merlin time. What do I do, Ophelia, what do I *do*?

Go deep? Somewhere inside Zareen's commandeered head my friend was still lurking, but how could I reach her? I didn't have time to sit and commune with the elements, not while she was determinedly trying to claw out my eyes.

I tried anyway. I focused and I *listened*, and for a few seconds, I thought I had it. An echo of the Zareen I knew, something that *felt* like her. *Yes*. I grabbed hold of Zareen and I *pulled*.

And when that didn't work, I lost my shit for a moment and tried the age-old art of headbutting. Why, you might ask? Did I think I could shock the ghost out of her by sheer brute force?

Hey, it was worth a try.

She shrieked, so did I (headbutting *hurts*), and nothing changed, except that on the next swipe she got hold of my face. Her thumb shoved into my mouth and her fingers were in my eyes and I was *mad*.

'Oh, for goodness' *sake*—' I spat, and bit.

She shrieked again, and released me.

I took immediate advantage.

I opened my mouth and, with a wisp of Merlin-magick, amplified my typically dulcet tones to impossible volume. '*SILVESSEN!*' I roared, and the syllables split the air with the force of a thunderclap, echoing off the bowl of the sky. 'THIS IS SOMEWHAT CONTRARY TO THE SPIRIT OF OUR AGREEMENT, DON'T YOU THINK? PLEASE RECALL YOUR ESTEEMED COLLEAGUES TO A SENSE OF DECORUM OR WE DO NOT HAVE A DEAL.'

Jay shot past, high-tailing it to gods-knew-where. Pursued, a moment later, by Emellana and Indira, and then Jay came back around again.

Okay. Playing chicken with the glaistigs. That's one way to distract them.

'SILVESSSSSEEEN,' I screamed again, because Zareen wasn't much daunted by my voice-of-the-gods routine and was coming at me again. 'Don't make me hurt Zareen or *I WILL HURT YOU.*'

I would have, too, in that mood. It had been a difficult day, I was tired, and worst of all, I was *hungry.* And the carrier bags containing my carefully chosen repast were lying scattered in the street getting rained upon because Silvessen's miserable cronies fancied *a possession party*, I mean, who's got time for this?

Thankfully, I wasn't obliged to do either of those things because she'd heard me. Well, she could hardly help it.

Another voice rolled through the heavens, almost as thunderous as mine. 'Alaiona. Celaena. Fanessel. Desist.'

Zareen stopped dead. Behind her, Indira and Emellana came to an equally abrupt halt, so sharply they almost toppled over. All three shuddered convulsively, and then all three *screamed,* which was *super* fun.

And then all three of my colleagues and friends collapsed in the dirt.

'Thanks,' I muttered weakly, and dropped to my knees beside Zareen.

She was already coming around; her eyes were open, and when she looked at me I knew it was Zar because she was *angry.*

She came up spitting with fury. 'Bitches tricked me,' she snarled. 'And they teamed me, too, because they *knew* I was the threat. Let me at them.'

'Nope,' I said, planting a palm on her chest when she tried to jump up. 'Silvessen recalled them because walking your carcasses around rather contravened the terms of the deal we just made. I'm afraid forcibly exorcising her only friends would have much the same effect.'

Zareen's only response was a wordless snarl, but she made no further attempts to tear off in a murderous rage, so I let her be while I checked on Emellana.

'Why does my head hurt,' I heard Zareen mutter as I left her.

Em was on her feet by the time I reached her, brushing mud off her coat.

'I'm sorry,' I said. 'I feel like we shouldn't have left you.'

Unruffled as ever, she twinkled at me. 'Food was important. Where is it, by the way?'

'Over there.' I pointed. 'You seem remarkably unperturbed for a recently possessed woman.'

'It's happened before. Never pleasant, but you can get used to anything.' With which wisdom, she ambled away in the direction of food, leaving me to unhappy contemplation of her words.

What do you have to go through to get used to malevolent possession?

Did I want to know?

I did not.

I turned in search of Indira.

No need. Her big brother had her in a big hug, which was good, because even from here I could see she was drawn and shaking. Poor girl. She was so young, she'd had none of the experience Emellana benefited from.

'I shouldn't have left you,' Jay was saying, echoing my own words. 'If I'd been here—'

'If you'd been here, what?' Indira interrupted, and pulled away from him. 'What were you going to do?'

Jay seemed at a loss for an answer. Fair, because it was a really good question. 'I don't know,' he finally said. 'Something to protect you—'

Indira became icily dignified, unconsciously mirroring Emellana's gestures as she brushed herself down. 'Bad things happen sometimes. You can't prevent that.'

'Even so—'

'*No*. It isn't up to you to protect me from the world, and it wouldn't help me much if you could. How am I supposed to become competent myself if you never let me experience anything that might be challenging?'

'There's challenging, and then there's forcible possession by a dangerous spirit—'

'Jay.' Indira looked him dead in the eye, ice-cold. 'Resilience is the product of encountering adversity, and surviving. You *do* want me to grow into a strong and capable adult?'

There was no good comeback to that, and Jay didn't try. Wise man. 'Okay,' he said, 'I hear you. I'm sorry.'

She nodded, and that was that.

'Thanks for the hug,' she said. 'It helps.' And then both of them were looking around for me, and for food, possibly in that order or possibly not.

The mood as we tore through our repast was subdued. I don't know what had led any of us to expect a nice, easy mission; when did that ever pan out? But we had, and instead we'd been emotionally tortured, our wits were tested, our physical bodies were pushed to their limits (and beyond), and finally several of us had been used as sock puppets.

And we hadn't eaten all day. At least that was a problem we could fix.

We ate huddled inside one of the more intact of Silvessen's cottages, which at least kept the rain and some of the wind off us. But a half hour sitting in one place left us shivering with cold and very ready to be going home.

I made the last morsel of my second eclair last, savouring the sweetness and the cream.

And when it was finished, and the last drops of cooling tea drained, I — and Jay and Zareen and even Emellana — turned a hopeful look upon Indira.

'Let's have a look,' said she, rising (a little stiffly) to her feet.

She crossed the street and sat in the dirt next to the regulator, sat there for a while with her palms to the earth and her brain on some other plane of reality. I don't know what she was doing, but after ten minutes she stood up, made a hopeless and ineffectual attempt to wipe the mud off her trousers, and shrugged. 'It seems to be okay,' she said.

Which is as good a way of tempting fate as any I've ever heard, and she really ought to have known better.

Because that was when the horde of carnivorous unicorns showed up.

Okay, just kidding about the unicorns. What actually happened was *nothing*, which at that point could scarcely have surprised me more.

'It's okay?' I repeated dumbly.

Indira nodded. 'I think so. Nothing anomalous is going on, and it seems stable.'

'Can you... get it out of there?'

'No.'

'Milady won't be happy.'

Indira looked pained. 'I know, and I would prefer to remove it, but I can't.'

'So we leave it here.'

'Yes. It'll have to be checked regularly for a few weeks to monitor the results, tweak and recalibrate as necessary, but for now it's fine.'

'And we can go home.'

'Yes,' said Indira, and added, fervently, '*please*.'

18

EXPLAINING THE DANCE PARTY to Milady wasn't as hard as you might think. She's met me before.

'So the only conceivable way to avert total disaster and certain death was to challenge the tormented and wronged inhabitants of Silvessen to a dance battle,' Milady said, just to make sure she had it straight.

'Exactly,' said I.

It was the next day, which was nice, because we'd had a free evening before we'd been summoned to make our report. An evening in which to get clean, and warm, and fed (again), and hugged (thank you Jay), and then to sleep the deep, peaceful slumber of Society agents who aren't being mercilessly tortured by a quartet of unhappy glaistigs.

I had, however, been summoned particularly bright and early: it was barely seven o'clock, I hadn't had breakfast yet, and was it my imagination or was the light getting steadily brighter in Milady's tower-top interrogation room? Searingly bright, like I was under police questioning and nobody wanted me to feel very comfortable anytime soon.

I shifted nervously, and made myself stop.

'And this worked out... well,' Milady continued.

'I mean, we lost,' I admitted. 'But I sort of did that my own self, so it's not the same as actually being *beaten*, and the results were—'

'Ves,' Milady interrupted. 'You've committed us to single-handedly restoring an entire town to its former glory. A town uninhabited for centuries, I might add, with no functional buildings and a magickal status best described as *bleak*.'

'Yes! Isn't it an exciting opportunity?'

There was a long and awful silence.

I didn't even have my staunch and trusty comrades to back me up, because I'd been brought up here alone.

'It's not exactly *single-handed* when there are a couple of hundred of us at the Society,' I ventured. 'And I'd be happy to lead this project myself.'

'Cordelia Vesper,' said Milady, in a terrible voice. 'If you think I will be landing anybody else with this — *project*, you are very much mistaken.'

'Understood,' I said quickly.

'It is fortunate that some parts of the... necessary undertakings will dovetail, to some extent, with Orlando's proposed programme of magickal restoration via the regulator.'

'That's what I was hoping.'

'And the Troll Court may take an interest, considering that this restoration is similar to their hopes for Farringale.'

'Exactly!'

'As for the rest.'

I waited.

'Do you have the first idea what it will cost to rebuild a town, Ves?'

'Not really, but—'

'And this is a heritage site of historical interest, so we cannot merely level the town and build whatever we'd like. Each of those buildings will have to be carefully restored, and rebuilt in a fashion that's respectful to their origins. Which means special materials, expertise—' She stopped with a gasp, as though the mere thought of everything had exhausted her.

I waited in meek silence for her to continue.

And when that didn't work, I piped up with: 'We have people for that!'

Which, in my defence, was true. It wouldn't be the first time we'd had to intervene to save ancient buildings of magickal import, and among the permanent employees at the Society were a range of people with exactly the sorts of skills in woodcarving, thatching, stonemasonry and iron-working that Milady was talking about.

'And the materials?'

This was a question I didn't have a smart answer for, a fact I betrayed with a lengthy and unpromising silence.

'I'll think of something,' I finally said.

'I would consider it advisable that you do,' said Milady, still rather awfully, and I trailed away feeling chastened.

EXPLAINING THE DANCE PARTY to Ophelia was consid-erably more challenging.

I hadn't had the courage to face her straight after my grilling at Milady's hands, so I took refuge in the first-floor common room.

Where she found me, an hour later, nursing a cup of tea and staring sadly out of the window.

Tea, note. Not chocolate. Milady was definitely not quite pleased with me.

'You're back,' Ophelia observed, sitting down opposite me in the chair Jay usually occupies.

It wasn't that I was unhappy to see Ophelia; she's a nice lady. But I wasn't pleased to see her right then, before I'd had chance to recover from my undignified drubbing at Milady's hands. As I watched her sit down, cool and calm and full of questions, I may have actually quailed a bit.

I forced a smile. 'As you see. How are you?' At least the common room was empty apart from the two of us. Nobody else would have to witness my attempts to explain the inexplicable to Merlin.

'Very well, thank you,' she said serenely, but I didn't miss the narrow look she shot me as she spoke. As usual, she saw through me. 'Why don't you tell me what happened?' she went on.

I heaved a sigh, finished the dregs of my tea, and set down the emptied mug. 'So. Silvessen was uninhabited, except not quite so uninhabited as we were expecting.'

The story took a while to get through, rather longer than I'd had to spend recounting everything to Milady. This was partly because Ophelia had questions. Lots of questions.

'You did what?' came up fairly often.

And twice she said: '*Oh?*' in that dangerous way parents adopt while their children try to explain why they're covered in chocolate spread from head to foot (example entirely hypothetical, definitely not something drawn from the storied experience of Tiny Ves).

Jay came in while I was about halfway finished. Finding his chair occupied, he took the seat next to me instead, and sat there in supportive silence while I stumbled through the rest of the story.

When I was finished, Ophelia looked at both of us in silence.

Finally, she spoke.

'So you used the ancient magick of Merlin to hold a dance competition.'

I suppressed a sigh, and nodded. Take it like a queen, Ves. 'It seemed the best thing to do,' I offered.

Her eyes widened at that. 'Did it?'

'What would you have done?'

She just stared helplessly at me. 'I don't know,' she said. 'But definitely not *that*.'

I waited, but nothing else was forthcoming. She seemed shocked speechless.

'Ves did great,' Jay interjected. 'The mission objectives were fulfilled, a rapport was established with the incumbents of Silvessen and a deal reached which will be of mutual benefit. Above all, no one was hurt.' He smiled slightly, wryly, and amended that. 'Save for a few pulled muscles all round.'

Ophelia was shaking her head. 'To call it an unorthodox approach would not begin to cover it.'

'That's Ves for you.'

'I see that.'

The look on her face. I tried not to feel like she was experiencing a crushing regret at having picked me for her successor.

Her next words dashed those hopes.

'I chose you as the best candidate to inherit Merlin's magick. Would you like to explain to me how that's still true?'

I opened my mouth, and closed it again. I had a surplus of smart answers I could've given, but this was serious. For once, I had to be serious too. Why was I the right person to be the next Merlin?

Was I, even? I wasn't certain of that myself. How could I convince Ophelia?

In the end, Jay saved me.

'Permit me to point out a couple of things,' he said. 'For one, Ves has a boundless imagination and an inexhaustible supply of creative solutions to difficult problems.'

Ophelia snorted with laughter, which seemed favourable, and shook her head, which didn't. 'Demonstrably true.'

'And for another. Let's consider the hazards of this kind of a power handover. The greatest danger has to be that you'll pick someone who won't prove trustworthy. Someone who'll abuse Merlin's magick, turn it to ill effect. Someone who'll be corrupted by it. Right?'

The ghost of a smile crossed Ophelia's face. 'I see where you're going with this line of thinking.'

Jay smiled, too, much more widely. 'So you gave Ves the opportunity to test drive Merlin's magick, and what did she do? She figured out right away that she could use it to influence, if not outright control, other people's behaviour, but what does that mean to Ves? The idea that she could enslave people to her will wouldn't even occur to her, let alone interest her. There's no puppeteering, no power tripping, and definitely no bloodbaths. No, you give Ves awesome cosmic powers and what does she do? She holds a dance party. That's Ves. And that's why she's the right person to be Merlin.'

I felt tears pricking behind my eyes, and had to swallow a lump in my throat. I couldn't even speak, so Jay had to be contented with a look of heartfelt gratitude. He smiled back, his eyes lingering on my face with an expression of such tenderness I had to look away.

Ophelia digested Jay's words in silence for longer than I was comfortable with. I felt like my fate hung in the balance here; if she didn't accept Jay's argument, she'd take back all the beautiful, ancient magick and go find someone else to embody the archetype.

I wasn't deeply committed to becoming the next Merlin; my life would go on even if I was passed over for it. But failure stings. And besides, I had stuff to do with those powers. I had heritage to save, people to help, magick to revive.

'A dance battle.' Ophelia was shaking her head again, but then, to my intense relief, she began to laugh.

She laughed and laughed until tears streamed from her eyes, and when she'd finally finished laughing she said: 'I'll say this: your turn as Merlin is going to be a lot more colourful than mine.'

Colourful. Good point. I touched a fingertip to a lock of my hair, and with a wisp of magick I turned it into a fluid purple-blue ombre. 'I'll consider it a point of honour,' I told Ophelia, who smiled, so that was all right, then.

Later, when Ophelia had gone back to her cottage-out-of-time, Jay and I lingered a while in the common room. I had a great many things to do: arrange for a burial crew to tend to the remains of the deceased at Silvessen; negotiate with the Troll Court for assistance with the rebuilding, via Emellana; exercise my Yllanfalen contacts in hope of further aid; and figure out where in the world I was going to get a town's worth of rare and expensive building materials.

But I didn't feel motivated to work on any of it. I was tired, which was fair; yesterday was a long, long day, and I'd exercised my physical and magickal powers in all manner of unusual ways.

I was also feeling a little deflated. Nothing had turned out quite the way I was hoping, and I wasn't sure what to make of where I'd ended up.

I must have heaved a little sigh, for Jay looked over at me and said: 'All okay?'

I gestured at the emptied teapot. 'I can't remember the last time Milady gave me tea.'

Jay knew what that meant; he grimaced. 'You deserved chocolate, though.'

'I think it's the rebuilding that she's unhappy about. It is going to be expensive, for sure.'

'That's fair.'

'And it is *good* tea. I think there was even some cream in it.'

'Not entirely in the doghouse, then.' He smiled at me, in a way that was probably supposed to be encouraging. I tried to smile back.

Jay leaned forward, resting his elbows on his knees so he could give me one of his long, intense looks. 'Ves. I meant what I said. You did a great job.'

'Thanks.' I managed a better smile. 'I hope Orlando's happy with us, at least?'

'Reckon so. Indira vanished into the attic last night, and I haven't heard from her yet. They're probably up to their eyeballs in data.'

'That's good. Probably be another test mission going on soon.'

'Maybe. Indira's going to be busy monitoring Silvessen for a while yet. All we've established so far is that the regulator's basic functions appear to work. What the effects will be on the Dell is a whole other question.'

'So we'll all be busy down at Silvessen for a while yet, thanks to me.'

Jay smiled and shrugged. 'Yes, but I for one am looking forward to it. I don't think anyone's ever brought an entire town back from the dead before. And if we can do something like that at Silvessen, what does that mean for Farringale?'

I nodded. 'I'm hoping the Troll Court will see it that way, too, and help us out.'

'Em will get them on board.'

I tried to picture anybody standing up to a serenely determined Emellana and prevailing. I couldn't. Even Their Majesties were outmatched there.

'Em and Alban,' I amended. 'Pretty sure he'll support us.'

Jay frowned slightly, and hesitated over his next words. 'About Alban.'

'Yes?'

He straightened again and leaned back in his chair, watching me. I wasn't sure what for. 'Are you... are you and he definitely not—?'

He didn't seem disposed to finish the sentence, so I took a guess. 'Going to be a thing? No. Definitely not.'

He scrutinised me with a rather dark gaze. I couldn't read his expression. 'I'm sorry,' he said.

'Are you?'

'Maybe. Are you?'

I thought about it, but I didn't need to think for very long. 'A little,' I admitted. 'But not as much as I might have expected. I think I was... dazzled.'

'He is pretty dazzling.'

'I doubt it would ever have worked out.' Saying that out loud hurt, a little. Part of me had really wanted it to work out, but that was probably the dazzled and stupid part. 'Anyway,' I went on. 'I so rarely date. I don't have time, or... inclination, much.'

'Really? You don't want to date?'

'I know that sounds weird.' I tried not to feel defensive; it wouldn't be the first time someone's reacted badly to the idea. 'I don't hate dating, but it's a lot of trouble and I don't feel in need of a relationship.'

Jay nodded slowly. 'I see.'

'That's what I meant when I said I was dazzled. I was so swept away by Alban that I forgot who I am, for a little while.'

'And who is that?'

I hesitated.

'If I may ask,' Jay said quickly. 'I don't want to pry.'

I eyed Jay for a moment in silence. How much could I tell him? How much did I want to tell him?

'I'm fine on my own,' I answered. 'I know people say that and sometimes it isn't true, it's a pose adopted against the loneliness that comes from wanting a relationship and not finding one. But in my case it's the truth. I've never felt a strong drive to get into romantic or sexual relationships, and if I go through the rest of my life without one, I'll be happy with that.'

Jay just nodded, giving me space to say more, if I wanted to.

I found that I did.

'I don't think I feel... attracted to people, the way others do,' I said. 'Not even Alban. I mean, he's aesthetically delightful, and I might've liked to be kissed a bit, maybe, but that's... that's all.'

Jay nodded again, silent with a watchful attention which felt welcoming, not condemning. There was warmth in his gaze.

So I went on. 'It's hard to talk about, because... because people think that you must be broken, you know? They say you just haven't met the right person yet, or that you must be damaged somehow. And maybe I've wondered, sometimes, if they're right. You know how people talk about love and sex and soulmates — like it's the crowning experience of all of humankind — and I've felt, sometimes, like I must be missing out on all that magic and beauty and — that my life must be the poorer for it.

'So when Alban showed up and I was a bit starry-eyed over him I thought... maybe this is it, maybe this is the "right person" who'll change those things about me, and I'll finally learn what all the fuss is about. My life will finally be right and healthy and complete, in all the ways people talk about.

'But that didn't happen, because it isn't that I haven't met the magical person who'll change me. It's that I don't need to change. My life isn't broken and I'm happy as I am. So, no, I'm not too disappointed about Alban. I have a fantastic life and I don't need a romance to complete me.'

I realised as I was speaking that I was trailing into defensiveness after all, but hey ho. I'd said it.

And far from condemning me, or recoiling from me, or arguing with me, Jay was smiling. '*You're* dazzling,' he said. 'Never mind Alban. You're the complete package all by yourself, and I agree: you don't need a soulmate. Your soul's perfect as it is.'

That sunk in all the way down, and lighted a little glow around my heart. 'Thanks,' I managed, through a fresh wave of threatened tears. Twice in one day, I must be tired. 'It's not that I don't love people,' I added. 'I do. Deeply. You can love people completely even without sex or romance. I don't think they're the same things, at all.'

'I have no trouble believing that,' said Jay.

'So... why were you asking about Alban?'

'Um, well...' Jay looked away, looked back at me, shifted in his seat. Uncomfy. What can of worms had I opened? 'I had thoughts of... asking you to dinner. Or something. If you were free.'

'You mean if I wasn't hanging my heart on Alban like a coatrack.'

'Something like that. But if you don't want to date—'

'I'd like to,' I said quickly.

Jay hesitated, perhaps waiting for a "but something" to follow.

'That's it,' I clarified. 'I'd like to.'

A smile, somewhat relieved. 'Let's rephrase what I was going to ask,' he said. 'Would you like to have dinner with me with a view to developing a deeper relationship in a largely non-romantic way, and which certainly isn't intended as a prelude to sex?'

'Would that be... okay?'

'Completely. Wonderfully.'

I smiled, too — then stopped as a thought occurred to me. 'But wait. Weren't *you* dating someone?'

'Briefly. Not now.'

'I'm sorry.'

'I'm not. The idea was of interest to our parents, so we gave it a chance. But we found it wasn't of similar interest to us.' He shrugged. 'We're friends. It's okay.'

'And your parents are okay with that?'

'Of course. They aren't tyrants.'

'Dinner's on, then.'

Jay beamed. 'How about tonight? Are you too tired?'

'Tonight's great. I do have something I want to do before then.'

'Oh? Do you need backup?'

I shook my head. 'Thanks, but not this time.'

19

MY ERRAND WAS OF a peculiar nature. It related to employing my Merlin magick at Home, in ways that hadn't occurred to me to do before. Ophelia had only loaned me that power, but she had made no move to take it back, yet. We'd agreed on a week, so I had time.

And I had questions. Lots of them. I'd had questions ever since I had joined the Society, of course; everyone did. But I'd learned a lot since then, and I finally had an idea about the nature of our Home and how it worked.

And that being so, I was curious, so I had to test it. Right? Who could possibly resist temptation like that?

It couldn't be done just anywhere, though. I made my way, slowly and uncertainly, through the winding corridors of our beloved and enormous House, and after wrong turns aplenty (even superpowered, I still have to be me), I found myself at the door to House's favourite room.

I knocked.

'Dear House. I know it is a trifle rude to arrive uninvited and unannounced, but this is important. Would you be so kind as to let me in?'

Silence.

Then, a click. The door had unlocked.

I turned the handle, and went in.

The room stood quiet and empty. I closed the door behind me, and took a seat on one of the upholstered ivory chairs. A fire flared to life in the grate, and a comforting warmth began to permeate the October chill in the air.

I sat in comfortable silence for a while, enjoying the ambience of the parlour. The grandfather clock tick-tocked to itself in the corner, a peaceful sound, and I began to relax.

The portrait of the troll lady in court dress was still there, above the chair Emellana had lately occupied. I studied it more closely than I'd had occasion to do before. She was of Emellana's age, I judged: fairly elderly, but still spry. Her gown was an extravagant blue velvet creation, seventeenth-century in style, with a wealth of lace and ruffles and jewels. She was a court lady, no doubt about it. But: which court?

I looked around at the rest of the paintings. There were five more: two depicting figures in seventeenth-century dress, one male, black and Yllanfalen, one female, white and human. Another showed a young man with dark brown skin wearing the plain garb of an eighteenth-century tradesman. The final two depicted a little girl in a plain white Edwardian dress, and an elderly, blue-eyed lady in an eighteen-thirties day dress and sun bonnet.

The child's portrait didn't fit my theory, but the rest just might. My gaze lingered in particular on the older lady in the sun bonnet.

I closed my eyes. Time to listen; time to feel. I'd connected with the odd, old house at Silvessen in deeper ways than I'd ever connected with anything before; could I do the same at Home?

I sat there enveloped in near silence, breathing deeply, listening to every slight sound that reached my senses. The tick, tick of the clock. The soft crackle of flames in the hearth. I breathed in the dust of hundreds of years with every inhalation; I felt the softness of carpet under my feet and silk under my hands, a cold wind in my eaves, the chatter of birds sheltering from the weather somewhere under my roof. A comfortable babble of voices, the warmth of many bodies gathered under my embrace. The odd cocktail of smells from the kitchens, from the lab, from the surrounding woods and fields.

A knock came softly from somewhere; a door opened in response, and closed again. Not the parlour. Somewhere farther off.

I gathered my strength, and pushed gently against the door that had just closed.

It opened again.

'*Sorry,*' I gasped, surprised, and retreated, slamming the door behind myself again.

There was a pause.

'*Hello?*' I said into the silence.

I felt a palpable surprise exceeding even my own. Then a questing, curious touch on my senses, all my senses: they were exploring me.

'*I come in peace,*' I offered. '*I'm just— interested. In who you are.*'

An answer came, finally. *Merlin,* uttered a voice in the depths of my mind. *It has been a long time.*

'*I'm only a new Merlin,*' I explained. '*Brand new. I've been here at the Society for a while, though.*'

We know you, Cordelia Vesper.

We. That tallied with my suspicions.

I felt a rising excitement, and had to take a breath. Focus, Ves. Don't get overexcited and ruin everything. '*May I know who I am addressing? Are these your portraits?*'

The faces we once wore are here commemorated, answered the voice. *They are but echoes, now.*

'*Memories,*' I supplied.

Yes.

Time for the million-pound question.

'*You recognise me as Merlin. Is that because you are archetypes, too?*'

A fresh wave of surprise. *Not now,* came the answer.

'*Former archetypes. And when you passed on the role, and passed away, you chose to remain here.*'

Not all of us chose to remain. Some journeyed on.

I felt *thrilled*, the delight you get from solving a fiendishly difficult puzzle. For more than a decade, I'd wondered how House came to be so — animated. Everyone had. And now I finally had something like an answer.

The spirits of former archetypes resided here. They were haunting the House, after a fashion; the way the Greyer sisters had haunted their cottage after death, and the way the Yllanfalen women of Silvessen haunted the craggy old house on the edge of the town. Except, not like that. They didn't linger out of bitterness and rage, and they hadn't been enslaved. They were here because they had loved the House in life, and they chose to remain with it after death.

I thought of the painting of Cicily Werewode, the way some part of her spirit was bound into it. Probably some part of those arts was employed here, too. The people depicted were dead, and yet they weren't; they lived on, their consciousness laced through canvas and oils, through brick and stone and tile. Bound to the House, and to each other, but bound in love, not hatred.

'*Greetings,*' I said brightly. '*It's an honour to meet you. Which archetype did you embody, if I may ask? Were you all the same archetype, at different times? Or different ones? Is it the same one Milady currently embodies?*'

Too many questions. I knew it as I uttered them, but they poured out of me anyway. I was just so *interested*, and Milady was so maddeningly vague.

I felt a flicker of something like amusement. More than just a flicker. A wave of it, coming from everywhere at once.

So much curiosity, said a voice, and it felt like a different person speaking. *An enquiring mind.*

I hoped I wasn't imagining the approval that came with the statement.

'*I have more,*' I offered. '*Lots more.*'

There followed a pause. Were they thinking? Don't think, I silently pleaded. Just answer!

The next voice, though, was very recognisable to me. It sliced through my thoughts with enough force to give me a blinding headache. *Ves. Leave this alone.*

Milady.

Curses.

'*I'm sorry,*' I said quickly, and not altogether sincerely. '*Can't I ask?*'

It is rude to pry, came Milady's somewhat flabbergasting answer. *Kindly remember your manners.*

My *manners?*

I ground my teeth in silent frustration. I could see her point, more than I liked. I *was* poking and prying, trying to find my way through to secrets about Milady's identity which she hadn't chosen to share. I did not have that right.

Even so, it was maddeningly frustrating to have to leave it alone and back away. I was so close to solving the mystery!

I know, Ves, said Milady. *It is very disappointing. But I remain unmoved.*

I sighed, and relinquished the argument. I withdrew my senses from the dear old House, returning to the Ves I'd left behind: a pint-sized human with fabulous hair, slumped in an ivory silken chair. My limbs had gone dead in my absence; I shook life back into them, and took some care as I stood up.

I made a curtsey, to Milady and also to the various souls inhabiting the House. 'Thank you for your time,' I said, scrupulously polite. 'I'll show myself out.'

The door didn't quite slam shut behind me, but it did lock in a manner I'd term decisive.

I wouldn't be getting back into House's favourite room any time soon.

My last errand for the day was of a less pleasant nature. As if bearing Milady's disapproval (twice over) wasn't enough, I was going to have to put up with my mother's, too.

Oh well. I'd dropped myself in it, and had nobody else to blame.

I trailed back to my room, and picked up my phone.

Taking a deep breath, I dialled my mother's number.

She picked up after the first ring, taking me by surprise. Normally she ignores my calls. 'Cordelia. What do you want?'

'Can't I be calling just to say hel—'

'Don't bother. Get on with it.'

'Right. Fair cop. I've got a problem.'

'And?'

'Well, to be accurate I've created a problem.'

'And now you're making it my problem.'

'Sort of. A little bit. Are you disposed to help me or not?'

'Depends what it is.'

So I launched into the Tale of the Dance Battle yet again, though I offered Mother a somewhat curtailed version.

Despite this, the silence when I'd finished was liberally flavoured with incredulity.

'Yes, I know, I'm a complete screw-up,' I said, before she could have a chance to say it herself.

'Did it work?'

'Well, it did. More or less.'

'Then it wasn't a screw-up, was it?'

'Are you being supportive? Because I'm not sure I can take any more surprises today.'

'Did we get to the part where you tell me what you want yet?'

'Right. So Silvessen was probably an Yllanfalen town, and if we're going to rebuild it sensitively then we need Yllanfalen aid.'

'That can probably be arranged.'

'And materials. Lots of those.'

That gave her pause. 'I can't just spirit up sufficient building materials to reconstruct an entire town, Ves.'

'I know, but I'm stuck, so whatever you've got I'll take.'

'Noted. Oh, call your father.'

'What? Why?'

'Because it's his birthday tomorrow.'

'Right. I know stuff like that, of course, because I've had a long and rewarding relationship with him up until now.'

'Also, he's a stonemason.'

'He's what?'

'Did you not hear me, or are you just being difficult?'

A stonemason. Whose birthday was tomorrow. I realised afresh how little I knew about my father. 'I don't have his number,' I said.

'I'll send it. Tell him I told him to help you.'

'Will that work?'

'It will if he knows what's good for him.'

She hung up.

A moment later, my phone buzzed with a message. Dad's number unfurled across my screen.

All of this was rather unexpected. I took my time over saving his number to my contacts, and adding his name. Thomas Goldwell. Tom.

I was procrastinating, probably because I was nervous. He hadn't seemed super pleased to learn of my existence before, and though I had given him my number the one time I'd met him, he had yet to call me.

That suggested he didn't want anything to do with me, didn't it?

Still. I wasn't calling him to propose a happy family gathering. I was calling him to engage his professional services for Silvessen. Mostly.

The phone rang several times before he answered. 'Hello?'

I swallowed a flutter of nerves, and pasted on a smile. 'Hi. Thomas Goldwell? Tom? This is Cordelia Vesper. You might not remember me—'

'Of course I do,' he interrupted. 'Adult women claiming a near relationship with me don't show up every week.'

'Right. Well, Dad, I have to tell you happy birthday. For tomorrow. Mum said so.'

'Thank you.'

That seemed to be it, so I went on. 'Also, I hear you're a stonemason.'

'I don't practise the trade much any more, but I do have that skillset, yes.'

'Okay. Then I've got a job for you.'

'Oh?'

'It's important. We're restoring an Yllanfalen town, and we need people with the right skills and insight.'

'Interesting, but I'm busy.'

'Also, Mum said you have to help me.'

'She said what?'

'I'll quote: "Tell him I told him to help you, if he knows what's good for him." Those exact words.'

He might have sighed, or there might have been a passing gust of wind, I couldn't be sure.

'Fine,' he said. 'Tell me when and where.'

I was speechless with shock, too much to muster more than a strangled 'thank you' in reply.

He hung up on me without saying goodbye, demonstrating that he and my mother had at least one thing in common.

'Great,' I said into the phone. 'See you soon.'

I put my phone away, uncertain as to the state of my feelings.

Mum was helping me out, and she hadn't even argued that much.

And I would finally get to meet my dad again, even if he didn't seem too excited about it.

Things among Family Ves were looking up. Vaguely. A little bit.

Sod it. If I didn't need a husband, I didn't need a mother or a father either. I'd managed just fine without those things.

Still, a girl can hope. Right?

Right.

And in the meantime, there's Jay, who's everything my family isn't, and presently waiting to whisk me away to a dream dinner that I hadn't even been able to scare him out of.

I dismissed my mountain of problems from my mind, opened my wardrobe and devoted myself to choosing a dress.

Enough work, Ves. Time to enjoy life a bit.

Also By Charlotte E. English

Modern Magick

The Road to Farringale

Toil and Trouble

The Striding Spire

The Fifth Britain

Royalty and Ruin

Music and Misadventure

The Wonders of Vale

The Heart of Hyndorin

Alchemy and Argent

The Magick of Merlin
Dancing and Disaster

House of Werth

Wyrde and Wayward
Wyrde and Wicked
Wyrde and Wild